Second Chance in Maple Bay

A MAPLE BAY NOVEL

Brittney Joy

Brittney Joy/Horse Girl LLC
www.brittneyjoybooks.com

Publisher's Note: This is a work of fiction. Names, characters, places, and incidents are a product of the author's imagination. Locales and public names are sometimes used for atmospheric purposes. Any resemblance to actual people, living or dead, or to businesses, companies, events, institutions, or locales is completely coincidental.

Cover design by The Red Leaf Book Design / www.redleafbookdesign.com
Book Layout © 2017 BookDesignTemplates.com

Second Chance in Maple Bay / Brittney Joy; Horse Girl LLC -- 1st ed.
ISBN 9798524612038

Dedicated to Brock and Cade.
Family isn't always defined by DNA. Thank you for
blessing me with your love. Proud to call you my sons.
Love you tons.

CHAPTER ONE

In the small town of Maple Bay, each resident was known for the horse they rode or the truck they drove. Kat had neither. Not anymore. Instead, she was driving down the highway toward her hometown in the tiniest car she'd ever seen.

Two weeks ago, Kat had cursed herself when she finally booked her flight from Chicago to Minneapolis. Since she'd waited until the last minute, there were slim pickings when it came to rental cars, and now she was driving north on I-90 in a car the size of a pop can. Her rental car was a Smart Car with wheels no bigger than dinner plates. From the driver's seat, she could reach the front and back windows.

Her suitcase was stuffed directly behind her, barely fitting in the "trunk." And when she dared to push the car over sixty-five miles an hour, the whole thing rattled like it might explode. Each time a semi-truck passed, Kat was certain the tiny car would be sucked under the trailer. After almost four hours of white-knuckled driving, she was more than thankful to exit the highway toward Maple Bay.

"We're almost there." Kat smiled at her two dogs—Thelma and Louise. They stared at her from their travel carrier, which was belted into the passenger seat. Louise, a caramel-colored Chihuahua-terrier mix, looked ready for a nap. Thelma, on the other hand, wiggled in place. She was a chocolate-brown spotted Jack Russell—basically the equivalent of a rubber ball ready to bounce off the walls at any given second.

"We should have time to stop and pick up donuts." Both dogs caught the excitement in Kat's voice. Louise cocked an ear in agreement, like the discerning old lady she was. Thelma began dancing around on her stubby legs.

Now that she was off the highway, it was only a half hour's drive to town. That gave her time to stop for a maple bar at *Patty Cakes*, Maple Bay's donut shop. She salivated just thinking about it. How long had it been since she'd had one? At least a year.

"We'll get a baker's dozen," Kat told the dogs. "That way I can eat one and Mom won't scold me for ruining my dinner. And I'll share with you guys too." Thelma's whole body was now wiggling. Especially her stumpy tail. She barked, and Louise looked at her like she was a cheap drunk. Kat laughed.

Zooming down the road as fast as her pop can of a car would take her, Kat soaked in the rural landscape that never seemed to change. At least it hadn't changed in her thirty-six years. Sweet farmhouses and wide barns were peppered amongst sprawling corn fields and a grid of gravel roads. Vibrant green pastures were grazed by horses of all colors and black-and-white cattle. Autumn leaves added splashes of red and orange which highlighted the open space like bundles of poppy flowers. Northern Minnesota was a stark contrast to Chicago, and Kat hadn't realized how much she needed a break from the hustle and bustle of the city until that moment.

Taking a deep breath, she released the stress of the past few weeks. Kat had been dreading her brother's wedding, but maybe this was just what she needed. A little time and space. Room to breathe.

But Kat should've known better than to let her guard down. Even for two seconds. In the time it took her to release the air from her lungs, a suicidal deer appeared and meandered into the road. She had no idea where it came from, but it wasn't running. The buck looked to be on a Sunday stroll, in no hurry to get out of her way.

Her car barreled toward the deer like a bullet. Kat slammed on the brakes. She would've screamed if she hadn't wasted all her breath on a useless sigh. Tires squealed, but the sharp noise seemed to lull the deer into a state of hypnosis. Instead of running off, he stopped and stared like he was posing for a picture.

This is not how I want to die, Kat thought and made a split-second decision.

She jerked the steering wheel to the right. The car shot off the pavement, and Kat *did* manage a scream as the car careened through the ditch like a rickety rollercoaster. It plowed into a tilled field while she held tightly to the steering wheel, trying to keep the car from flipping.

When the car finally lurched to a stop, Kat immediately turned to her dogs. She peeled her fingers from the steering wheel and nearly cried when she confirmed her babies were safe.

"Thank you, Jesus, Mary, and Joseph." She made a quick sign of the cross.

Both dogs were at the front of the carrier, next to soft padding, where they'd been propelled. Kat checked them over and gave them each kisses on their furry heads. Then she started to assess her situation.

"Oh my goodness." Kat pushed open the door and started to get out of the car before fully thinking through her decision. Her mind was a mess, and as she stepped out of the car, her foot became a mess too. A muddy mess, to be exact.

That morning, before heading to the airport, Kat had stopped at her office to finish up a few loose ends before heading home for the week. Now, as her foot sank into deep mud, she wished she'd changed out of her work clothes before getting on the plane. High heels, dress slacks, and a cashmere sweater weren't doing her any favors in the country.

Kat squeaked and instinctively yanked her foot back toward the car. Instantly, she regretted her move. The mud suctioned her shoe off and squirted slop across the front of her sweater. Kat cursed, hoping she'd reached her quota of bad luck for the day.

"Oh, for real." She stared at her muddy, bare foot, not sure what to do next.

Then, as if to rub salt in her wound, the deer that had caused her to catapult into this slop field leisurely walked back to where he had come from, like he didn't really need to cross the road in the first place. Kat was glad she hadn't hit the deer, but his blatant disregard for her safety—and his own—irked her.

"Maybe next time you could look both ways before you cross?! Huh?!"

The deer trotted off, not acknowledging her suggestion.

Frustrated, Kat shook her foot, trying to dispel some of the muck. It didn't go anywhere, and she knew the same would be true for her rental car. There was no way it could drive out of this, even if it started. Mud was halfway up the wheels.

She sighed and looked for her phone. The sun was setting and the temperature dipping. Before long, she'd need to pull clothing out of her suitcase and layer-up to stay warm. She could call her dad or one of her brothers for a ride, but Kat's heart fell when she laid eyes on her phone. It was on the floor next to the gas pedal. The screen was black and cracked like a spiderweb.

"No, no, no." She picked it up, only to find it wouldn't turn on. "You can't do this to me. Why are you so fragile?" For as much money as she'd paid for the phone, it should be shatterproof, waterproof, *and* lose-proof. Just like the deer, her phone had no answer for her. She hastily set it down.

Kat turned to Thelma and Louise. They were now looking at her with concern. "Looks like we're going for a walk." And by that, Kat meant she'd put on her coat, gloves, and hat. Then she'd tuck her two dogs into the front of her coat where they would curl against her chest and stay warm. She'd walk them all to the closest house and ask to use a phone. But as she reached behind her seat, awkwardly trying to retrieve her coat from her suitcase, Kat noticed a truck slowing to a stop on the road. She immediately recognized it and cursed under her breath. The 1985 black Chevy dually brought back a plethora of memories that went back to high school.

The man driving the truck did too.

Kat scrambled forward and stared out the windshield again. Her heart thudded against her ribs. She'd successfully avoided Creed Sheridan for five years, but now he was a groomsman in her brother's wedding. There was no way to avoid him this week. She knew that. She just hadn't expected to run into him before she even got to town . . . in the middle of a tilled corn field, sitting in a broken car, practically dipped in mud.

She wasn't ready to see him.

Setting her forehead against the top of the steering wheel, Kat gathered her thoughts. What was she to do? Shut the door, lock it, and pull her coat over her head? She considered it. After all, Creed wouldn't have a guess as to who would be driving a silver Smart Car. She could hide if she wanted to. But then she'd still be stuck in the mud.

Kat raised her head, unprepared for this encounter, and when she saw herself in the rearview mirror, she yelped. Somehow, she'd smeared mud across her forehead.

"Hey! You okay in there?" Creed yelled. He must've heard her call of distress and thought she was hurt instead of reacting to an unwanted mud facial.

Kat closed her eyes tight, knowing she had to face him. Abruptly, she turned and leaned out the open door. "I'm okay." She waved her hand like all was good. Like this was normal. Like she meant to drive out into the mud.

Creed was halfway between his truck and her car, trudging through the mud. When she made herself visible, he stopped like he'd just seen a ghost. "Kat?"

"Yep, it's me." She gave him an uncomfortable smile. "I'm fine. Just tried to avoid a deer and ended up going on an involuntary cruise."

He looked just as she remembered him—tall, blond, and built like a quarterback. Except instead of a jersey and cleats, he sported jeans, a gleaming oval belt buckle, and a button-down shirt with the sleeves rolled up to his elbows. She was a hundred percent certain cowboy boots were hidden beneath the muddy hems of his pants. The only thing missing was his perfectly cocky smile.

Creed started walking toward her again. "Are you sure you're okay? Looks like you really went flying." He looked back, and his eyes followed the tire marks that skated through the field.

"Yeah, I'm fine." Kat tucked her hair behind one ear. When she realized she'd added a streak of mud to her hair, she rolled her eyes at herself. "It's just that I'm kind of stuck now."

"Uh, yeah." Creed gave a huff. "I'm surprised that go-kart of yours made it that far. It's not made for off-roading." He gave her a smirk. Kat tilted her head at him, annoyed.

"It's a rental." When Kat lived in Maple Bay, she'd had a truck of her own. Her rental car could've fit in her truck's bed. Now, she didn't even own a car. She could get wherever she needed in Chicago by hopping on the train or grabbing an Uber. Her truck days were long gone. She was a different person now, one Creed couldn't possibly know, especially if he was going to get all smirky. "Don't worry about me, though. I was just going to call Evan. He'll come and get me." Kat's mind was flashing all kinds of caution signs right now, and she'd say just about anything to make Creed go away.

Creed furrowed his brow. "Why don't you just come with me? You're going to the same dinner I am."

Kat's heart squeezed. Of course Creed would be at Sunday dinner tonight. She wasn't surprised, but no one in her family had thought to give her a heads-up?

Creed's smirk fell away. "Kat, I'm not going to leave you out here. What do you need me to grab? A suitcase? We can leave your car. Evan and I can come back in the morning with a trailer. I'll call old man Miller. I'm sure he'll let you park in his field overnight. Besides, you know your family would have my head if I left you stranded here."

Kat considered her options. *Accept a ride with Creed? Walk to a nearby house and call Evan? Hitchhike? Take a super long walk to her parents' house?*

Just then, Thelma barked.

Creed cocked his head and closed the distance to her car. He peered in. "Did you bring your dog?"

"Dogs. Plural." Kat glanced at Thelma and Louise. They were staring at her longingly from the carrier. Both were shaking. That was her tipping point. She would happily endure the cold to avoid close quarters with Creed. But she wouldn't inflict that on her dogs. Sighing, she looked back at Creed. "Okay. Could you grab my suitcase out of the trunk?"

"Yeah." Creed slopped through the mud to the back of the car and opened the hatchback. As he pulled her suitcase from the trunk, Kat freed the dog carrier from the seatbelt.

He gestured toward the road. "I'll put your suitcase in my truck and be right back to help you with the rest."

"I've got it. It's just my dogs and my purse."

"You sure?"

"I'm sure. I got it. I'll be right behind you."

Creed closed the hatchback, and Kat reached for her purse, which was toppled over on the floor. Thankfully, it was zipped shut, the contents contained. Quickly, she opened it and dug into the tiny pocket on the side. When she found her engagement ring, she yanked it out and pushed it back on her finger.

With a deep breath, Kat hooked the dog carrier over her shoulder. Then she kicked off her clean shoe and slid out of the car. Barefoot in the cold mud, she unwillingly sloshed toward her ex-boyfriend's truck.

CHAPTER TWO

The drive to Kat's childhood home would take maybe fifteen minutes, but the charged tension inside the truck made each second feel like an hour. The dogs sat in their carrier on the bench seat between Kat and Creed. Kat was thankful for the barrier.

"Thanks for the ride," Kat broke the silence. Her arms were wrapped around her purse, pressing it to her stomach like a shield. Louise stared at Kat under shaggy, wiry eyebrows like she was telepathically asking if they'd been kidnapped. Thelma was wiggling her brown-spotted butt, looking at Creed like he might give her a treat. *Traitor.*

"Do your parents know you crashed your car?" Creed asked before turning onto the road that ran along the jutted edge of Maple Leaf Lake.

"No. I hadn't had a chance to call anyone before you stopped." Kat cringed, reminded of the fact that her phone was broken. She needed it in order to stay on top of work emails this week. Otherwise, she'd be chained to her laptop. She really didn't want to imagine how her boss would react if she couldn't get ahold of Kat in an emergency. And everything was an emergency to Wendy.

Kat would have to buy a new phone. She'd order it and ship it overnight.

Creed shifted in his seat and pulled a handkerchief from his back pocket. "Here. You've got some schmuck on your face."

Releasing her death grip on her purse, Kat accepted his handkerchief. "Schmuck might be an understatement. Not exactly how I wanted to show up for dinner." Kat pulled down the sun visor and looked in the mirror. It looked like she'd been fighting with a pig. Using Creed's handkerchief, she blotted and scrubbed at the mess on her forehead.

"Congratulations, by the way," Creed said, seemingly out of nowhere. Kat glanced at him and had a split-second flashback to the many hot summer nights she'd spent in this truck. *Creed laughing. The windows rolled down. Driving to nowhere.*

"On the engagement," he added.

Kat realized he was staring at her ring finger. "Oh. Thank you." Her eyes shot back to the mirror. Her fingers scrubbed at her forehead a little harder.

"He didn't come with you? For Jesse's wedding?"

Kat kept scrubbing. "He couldn't get out of work, but he'll be here later."

Michael worked in human resources for the same company as Kat. They'd been dating for the past two years. Two months ago, he proposed. Michael's heart was the size of a watermelon. He was kind, reliable, and motivated. He volunteered with Kat at the animal shelter. He gave her a bouquet of roses every Friday. He loved his momma. He was everything she needed in a partner, and the complete opposite of Creed. Kat didn't understand why she'd been panicking ever since he proposed.

Creed made an agreeable sound somewhere deep in his throat.

"He's flying in on a red-eye," she lied. "He'll be here early on Saturday."

The ring tightened on her finger. Like a noose.

"It's a big ring," Creed said, like she was wearing a tutu around her forehead.

Kat wasn't sure what to make of that and chose to ignore it as they arrived at her parents' house. She didn't want to discuss Michael or her ring, especially with Creed.

Instead of responding, she looked ahead, down the long gravel driveway to the cherry-red Victorian farmhouse that was her savior. Warm light radiated from white-trimmed windows, and a fleet of trucks lined the driveway. It was nearly six o'clock, and Kat knew her family would be anxiously awaiting her arrival. All her siblings, their kids, and significant others would be here. Plus, there would be cousins, aunts, and uncles. After all, it was Sunday. Sundays always started with church and ended with a big family supper.

Speaking of supper, Kat intended to cram her mouth with plenty of home-cooked food. If her mouth was full, she might be able to avoid all questions about Michael, her engagement, and a future wedding date. Though she doubted that. The Weston women had a way of dragging the truth out of anyone. It would be a miracle if she made it through this week without spilling the beans.

Keep your answers simple. Deflect, deflect, deflect.

Creed parked at the back of the pack. "I'll get your suitcase." He got out of the truck before Kat could reply.

Kat opened her door and hopped out, putting her muddy, bare feet on the gravel. She leaned back into the truck to grab the dog carrier. Sliding it out, she placed it on the grass and opened it. Louise hopped out and sniffed a blade of grass. Thelma bounced out like a bunny and raced around Kat in a circle.

"Where do you want this?" Creed asked. Kat looked up. He was standing at the front of his truck, holding her suitcase. The sight of him in front of her childhood home hit her harder than she expected, and a rush of memories grabbed her.

Cheering for him at every rodeo. Secret rendezvous at the lake. Snuggling in his truck. Countless stolen kisses and shared dreams.

Creed was her first love. He'd also broken her heart. A couple of times.

Kat shook her head. "Just leave it there. I'll get it."

"Kat." Creed spoke her name in protest but closed his mouth when the front door burst open. Kat's mom spilled out. Her dad was right behind.

"Oh, for goodness' sake!" her mom yelled. Joyce zoomed toward Kat, her arms out, ready for a hug before she even left the porch. "Katherine Marie Weston! What happened? Where have you been? We were so worried! Why didn't you call?"

Kat wasn't sure which question to answer first, but Joyce snatched her into a hug and pressed Kat against her hefty, apron-clothed bosom. Kat sank into her mom's embrace and soaked up her scent. Somehow, her mom always smelled like sugar cookies.

"Sorry." Kat wrapped her arms around her mom's shoulders and squeezed tight, hoping her apology was felt through her hug. "My stupid rental car broke down." She left out the part about narrowly avoiding a deer and shooting into a mud field at sixty-five miles an hour.

Kat's father joined them. Gene was wearing his signature outfit—a plaid flannel and suspenders that kept his jeans securely in place. "Your car broke down?" he asked in concern.

Joyce pulled back and looked at her daughter. Her short silver hair was tightly curled with a fresh perm. "What's with the mud?" Joyce asked, before Gene pulled Kat into a hug.

"Got stuck." Kat mumbled into her dad's chest. It was the best explanation she could give that wouldn't get her parents riled up. When her dad let her go, she explained, "It was just outside of town. Creed was driving by when it happened. He gave me a ride."

Her mother's eyebrows shot up. She looked toward Creed, but he wasn't standing near his truck any longer. He was at the front door, taking off his boots. He had Kat's suitcase.

"Well, good thing Creed was there," her dad said. He gave Kat one more squeeze around her shoulders. "Let's get you inside and cleaned up. Everyone's waiting for you."

As Creed disappeared into the house, Kat's brother Jesse burst out the door. "There's my little sister!" He jogged toward her, and the big smile on his face was contagious. Kat returned it.

Jesse hugged her, pulling her off her feet and spinning her around. She laughed, and by the time he set her down, Kat's oldest brother, Evan, had joined the hug. Thelma barked and ran more circles in the grass.

"Oh," Joyce cooed. "It's *so good* to have all my babies home."

The warmth in Joyce's voice could've melted a Minnesota winter, but as Kat eased back from her brothers' embrace, she felt a sharp stab at her heart. The Weston kids were all close in age. Jesse was two years older than Kat. He'd be thirty-eight when he married his bride this Saturday.

Evan was barely a year older than Jesse. Being so close in age, they were always mistaken for twins. Plus, her brothers shared the same tall frames, dark hair, and ice-blue eyes. Their sister, Anne, was the oldest, but only a year older than Evan.

And their youngest sister, Sarah, Kat would never see again.

She swallowed, pushing away the unwelcome pain.

Jesse must've caught the struggle on her face, because he scooped her in close and started walking toward the house. "What were you doing? Playing football? You're a mess," he teased. He shook her shoulders until a small grin surfaced on Kat's face. "There, that's better. We're so glad you're here."

Kat set her head against her brother's chest and pushed away the pain. "Of course I'm here. You're getting married, Jesse," she said. This was going to be a happy week. There was no time for tears. She could cry when she got back to Chicago.

Kat stepped into the kitchen, and a flurry of commotion ensued. The room was packed with at least fifteen family members, and they all cheered at her entrance. Kat braced for the barrage of hugs. Her cousin Myra got to her first, squeezing her and squealing, telling Kat she was so excited to spend the week with her. Kat was excited to see her too, but only got two seconds to tell her so because the crowd closed in. Aunts. Uncles. More cousins. Her grandpa. There were hugs galore. No one seemed to care about the mud that decorated Kat's body.

When she broke free of the hug-train, Kat spotted her sister, Anne. She was at the stove, wearing an apron, looking like she couldn't leave the steaming pots.

Anne waved Kat over. "Come here, sis."

"Hey, Anne." Kat gave her sister a hug, avoiding the wooden spoon Anne held on to.

"Glad you could join us," Anne said with a smile, though there was a reprimand in her eyes. "Your nieces and nephews miss you. They're all outside, playing kick-the-can, if you want to say hi."

From anyone else, the same words wouldn't have bothered Kat. But coming from Anne, Kat knew they were intended as a reminder—that Kat needed to be a better daughter, sister, and aunt. She needed to call and visit more often. That she should've never moved away.

"Missed you too," Kat replied and genuinely meant it. Then she turned to the big kitchen island and looked for something to stuff into her mouth. There was no shortage of options. Crockpots, casserole dishes, and serving bowls boasted all the savory and sweet goodies Kat had been looking forward to. She snatched a dill pickle from a bowl. The pickle was smeared in cream cheese and wrapped in corned beef. It was an appetizer Joyce made at every family gathering. The pickles were usually gone well before dinner, so Kat was glad there were still some left.

As soon as the pickle was in her mouth, Jesse and his fiancée, Hazel, appeared from the living room.

"I'm so sorry," Hazel said, grabbing Kat into a hug. "I was on the phone with the florist, making sure everything is wrapped up for the wedding. How are you?"

"Good." Kat chewed quickly, not wanting to talk with a mouthful of pickle. Especially because she already looked like a disaster. She swallowed. "And, no worries. I bet you have a ton of stuff going on. Let me know if I can help with anything." She had only met Hazel once, when Kat was in town the previous Christmas, but she had known right away that Hazel was the one for Jesse. Jesse practically turned into the heart-eye emoji around Hazel. He was happy and at ease, and Kat was thankful that her brother had found his other half.

"Oh, I appreciate the offer," Hazel said, tucking her phone into her pocket. "There's so much going on this week. It's so nice to have all the help from everyone."

"Just let me know. I'm here all week, so I'm happy to help with anything," Kat offered, even though she knew she was going to have to squirrel away to get her work projects done in between wedding stuff. At that thought, her anxiety amped up and she snatched a garlic cheese curd from the smorgasbord. She popped it in her mouth. As it squeaked between her teeth, the sliding glass door that led to the back deck slid open. A woman Kat didn't know walked in and practically bounced along the edge of the kitchen, looking like she knew exactly where she was going. As she moved through the archway and into the living room, she squealed, finding her target.

Creed.

He had just come down from upstairs, and the woman jumped on him, wrapping herself around him like a little monkey. He kissed her, and Kat was surprised . . . but not really. The woman was just his type. She was petite, had long, bleached-blonde hair, and her breasts threatened to pop out the top of her shirt at any given second. As Creed held the spry woman up by the seat of her jeans and kissed her, Kat's stomach flipped. She blamed it on the over-the-top display of PDA instead of admitting to herself that she'd never been able to suppress the twinge of jealousy that came when she saw Creed with someone else. She couldn't believe that feeling was still there, lurking inside her, waiting to jump out and remind her—

"Yeah, Kat could totally do that," Jesse said, and Kat snapped out of her trance. She had been staring at Creed so intensely that she'd completely missed the last bit of conversation.

"Huh?" Kat said, realizing both Jesse and Hazel were looking at her, waiting for some type of response.

"Pick up the bridesmaid dresses tomorrow," Jesse said. "That would really help free up our time to get a few other things done."

"Oh, yeah. Totally. I can do that." Kat needed to go to Eleanor's seamstress shop anyhow. Eleanor had sewn Kat's dress solely from the measurements Kat had given her mother. She needed to try on the dress to make sure no last-minute alterations were needed.

"That'd be great." Hazel heaved a grateful sigh. "Thank you."

"Of course. It's no problem," Kat replied.

Jesse jerked a thumb toward Creed, who had, thankfully, stopped making out with the mystery woman and was now joining the conversation. "Creed can pick you up at nine," Jesse said.

Creed looked like someone had elbowed him in the stomach. Kat was sure she looked the same but cleared her throat to distract her face from revealing her true feelings about Jesse's suggestion.

"Pick up Kat?" Creed asked.

"Who's Kat?" asked the blonde hanging on Creed's arm.

Kat kept her face even. "I'm Kat." She offered her hand to the blonde woman. "Jesse's sister."

The blonde woman flushed. "Oh, how embarrassing. I'm sorry. You're Kat . . . Katherine, right? I'm Zoey." She shook Kat's hand.

"Nice to meet you, Zoey." Kat smiled, not intending to embarrass the woman. Maybe she was a new girlfriend? Or a new fling. Whatever Creed did these days. Kat turned to Jesse. "It's fine. I can drive myself." Her rental car may have been out of service, but she could take her mom's car or her dad's truck. She would drive the tractor if she had to.

"Creed's going to Eleanor's anyhow. He didn't get fitted for his suit last week like he was supposed to." Jesse gave Creed a playful eyeroll. "Just had to get in one more rodeo, didn't ya?"

One more rodeo? Of course he did.

"I've got to go anyhow. I can pick you up at nine," Creed offered, echoing Jesse's instructions. The blonde woman gave Kat a look that felt a little judgmental.

Kat wanted to protest, but her Aunt Judy called across the kitchen island. "So, Kat, when's *your* wedding date? Better pick one soon if you want Jake's to cater it. I hear their calendar is filling up fast."

All eyes turned to Kat, and she managed a tight smile. "Probably summer," she babbled. "But we haven't picked a date yet."

"Don't you go off and elope now," her grandpa, Vern, added. "You know how I like a party."

Kat chuckled awkwardly at his humor. He did like a party. He was nearly ninety and had a livelier social life than she did. "Of course not, Gramps."

He gave her a wink and an approving nod.

"Oh, my goodness. You'll be the next bride," Hazel said, truly excited. "Have you looked at dresses yet?"

Deflect, deflect, deflect.

"Not yet." Kat quickly shook her head. "Speaking of clothes, I should really change." She whistled for her dogs. Thelma hopped through the crowd to join Kat at her muddy feet. Louise stared at Kat from the comfort of her dad's arms. She was curled up against his suspenders, nearly asleep.

"I'll take her, Dad," Kat said, and held out her arms. "They're probably hungry. I'll feed them and change into some clean clothes."

Her dad handed Louise over like she was a baby. "Okay, but you better bring her back so she can cuddle with me on the couch after dinner." Gene smiled.

"Of course." Kat loved that her parents treated her dogs like they were furry grandchildren. She started walking toward the guest room, which was next to the master bedroom on the main level.

Creed put his hand on Kat's arm, startling her. "Your aunt told me to put your suitcase upstairs. I guess your great-aunt Viola will be staying in the guest room."

Kat's vision traveled up Creed and hit his forest-green eyes. "Upstairs?"

The second floor held three bedrooms and one bathroom. Growing up, Jesse and Evan shared a room. Anne had her own. Kat had always shared with her baby sister, Sarah. Kat hadn't stayed upstairs since she moved to Chicago. When she came to visit, she always stayed in the guest room. It had a queen bed, generic farmhouse décor, and no memories that could rip her to shreds.

"I put your suitcase in the boys' old room." Creed's eyes told Kat that he knew what she was thinking.

Kat paused for a beat, clenching Louise closer to her chest. Then she straightened and nodded. She moved past Creed and started up the stairs. Thelma followed, clicking up the wooden stairs, but all Kat could focus on was the door at the top of the staircase. She was glad it was closed, because she wasn't ready to face her old bedroom. She'd already faced Creed and couldn't handle more heartbreak. Not today. So she bypassed the closed door and headed down the hall to her brothers' old bedroom.

This was going to be a long week.

CHAPTER THREE

The next morning, Creed showed up early to the Weston house. As he stepped into the mudroom from the garage, he heard Kat talking. He'd tried to call her, to tell her he'd be early, but his call had gone straight to voicemail. Frankly, he'd half-expected Kat to blow him off this morning, a feeling confirmed when she avoided his call. She'd been avoiding him for years. What was one more day?

Creed stepped into the kitchen, expecting Joyce to be with Kat, finishing her last cup of coffee for the morning. Instead, Kat was standing at the kitchen island, alone and talking to herself. Was she on the phone? Maybe that's why she hadn't answered his call. Kat's back was to Creed, and her barely-there athletic shorts gave him pause. He couldn't help but take note of her long, toned legs. They'd never failed to capture his attention.

"Good morning," he said, forcing his eyes up.

Kat jerked at the sound of his voice. When she looked at him over her shoulder, he saw a computer screen. There was a laptop in front of her on the island, and a bunch of little faces stared back at him.

"Crap," Creed muttered. Kat was on a video call, probably for work, and now he was making a guest appearance. Creed jumped to the side and out of the camera's reach. From his new spot close to the sink, he mouthed "Sorry."

"Katherine?" a high-pitched female voice sang out of the laptop and grabbed Kat's attention like a police siren. "What's going on? Finish your thought. I have another call in two minutes. Actually, I have calls scheduled all day, so I need to make sure this is taken care of before I get off this call. I won't have a spare second to talk to you later today."

Kat diffused the shock on her face. "Absolutely, Wendy." Kat looked straight at the laptop like she'd transformed into a robot. "I've got this handled. I'll tweak the reports like we talked about and send them to you by end of day so you can review the changes when you have time."

"By end of day, Katherine," the woman repeated like she was scolding a child. "There's no room for error. Get all of those changes made, and we can review this again tomorrow."

"I understand. I'll get it done right away."

"I'll be waiting," the voice trilled before the screen went black and Kat fell onto the counter like a deflated balloon.

"She sounds like a *peach*." Creed leaned against the sink. "Your boss?"

"Ugh, yes." Kat's face was still planted on the counter. "She drives me crazy." She lifted her head and stood. "Sorry, I meant to be ready when you got here. I went for a run and when I got back, my boss surprised me with a group video call. I've got a big presentation next week for an account I've been trying to land for the past year. And I'm up for a promotion. I've got a lot going on right now with work." Kat made a few quick keystrokes on her computer, not looking at him.

Creed crossed his arms, still leaning against the white farmhouse sink. "That's good, right?" Kat had always been insanely motivated and whip-smart. It didn't surprise Creed that she was excelling at her job. From what he'd heard from her parents and brothers, she'd quickly climbed the corporate ladder.

Kat typed away, and as Creed waited for her to answer him, he realized her running shorts were topped off by a pressed, collared shirt. She must've thrown it on when she found out about the work video call.

"Yeah." Kat finally responded and closed her laptop. "I just wish I had more time to get it all done."

"If you need some time to work, I can go pick up the dresses and suits."

Kat looked like she was considering his offer but then shook her head. "No, I need to try on my dress to see if it needs alterations. Thanks, though." Creed wasn't certain if her obvious irritation was related to work or to him. "Can you give me five minutes?"

"Sure."

Kat tucked her laptop under her arm and grabbed the notebook next to it that contained a whole page of notes. Then she trotted off upstairs. Creed wandered into the living room where Kat's dogs were curled up into little balls on the couch.

"Hey, guys," Creed said. The friendly one—Thelma— unballed and wiggled around until Creed petted her. His hand engulfed her little, round head and rolled down her body. Thelma closed her eyes in adoration of the full body rub. The scruffy dog—Louise—opened one eye, but otherwise didn't move. Creed scratched the top of her head anyhow. "You two have a long day yesterday? Tuckered out?"

As he continued rubbing and scratching the little dogs, Creed's eyes wandered to the quilt and pillow they were snuggled up against. He immediately recognized both. Joyce had sewn the quilt and matching pillowcase for Evan for his sixteenth birthday. They were covered in football images and had been on Evan's old bed when Creed had set Kat's suitcase in the bedroom last night.

Kat jogged down the stairs and appeared in the living room, wearing jeans and a sweater. Her honey-blonde hair was pulled back into a tight bun.

"Did you sleep on the couch last night?" Creed asked, even though he knew he shouldn't have. Especially when Kat stiffened at his question.

"Just got up early," she replied abruptly. "It was cold, so I brought the quilt down. You know how Dad likes to keep the house at sixty overnight. You ready?"

Creed didn't buy Kat's response. Joyce had a million afghans and quilts. There were at least five in the living room, draped over the back of the couch and both recliners. But he didn't press. Kat hadn't talked to him in years, and the last time they'd been together, she'd made it perfectly clear that Creed had no place in her life.

Yesterday, when Creed had stopped on the side of the road, concerned for whoever had veered off the highway and into a field, he'd never expected to find Kat. He was on his way home from a rodeo in Bismarck, North Dakota. The entire drive he'd been thinking of what he'd say to Kat when he saw her at supper that night. A simple "hello" or "how are you?" wouldn't do. He wanted to make things right with Kat. They would never be together as a couple. Creed had blown all chances of that. Now, he just wanted to be friends. He wanted Kat to feel comfortable around him again.

Creed stood and followed Kat outside, and they got into his truck for another uncomfortable drive. Creed tried to make small talk, but Kat shut him down with one-word answers. When they got to Main Street—the road that separated Maple Bay's downtown businesses from the lake—Creed tried to think of a subject to get Kat talking. As they passed *Kandi's Candy Shop*, Kandi waved excitedly from the window. Both Creed and Kat waved back. As they did, Kat's engagement ring sparkled in the sun.

Creed looked back at the road, away from the ring. "I'm looking forward to meeting Michael," he said, and immediately wished he'd picked a different topic. Did his statement sound as stupid as he thought it did? "At the wedding."

Kat placed her hand back in her lap. "He's excited to get here."

She toyed with her ring, twisting it around on her finger, and Creed thought again how the ring didn't match Kat. At least, not the Kat he knew. The diamond was huge and jutted out from the band. Kat had always been active, a self-proclaimed tomboy. She rivaled Creed and her brothers on four-wheelers and snowmobiles. Kat could ride a horse with the best of them, and she loved playing sports—baseball, kickball, volleyball, even football. Could she do any of those things while wearing that ring? Creed was certain the diamond would gouge someone like a knife. Maybe she just didn't do any of those things anymore?

"How'd he propose?" Creed had already heard the story from Joyce one too many times during Sunday dinners. Kat had said *yes* in a restaurant on the top floor of a Chicago skyscraper. Like the ring, the proposal didn't fit Kat either.

When Kat didn't respond, Creed glanced over, wondering if he'd gone too far. Was it wrong that he wanted to hear about Michael from Kat's mouth? That he wanted to witness the expression on Kat's face and know that she was happy? That he wanted to let go of her but couldn't until he knew she was better off?

Kat's mouth was parted. Her eyes looked tired, like she needed a good night's sleep or a gallon of coffee. He didn't see the bright glow of happy love in her hazel eyes, the eyes he knew so well. But before she responded, Creed's phone rang. It sat on the seat next to his thigh, and when he glanced down, the screen said the call was from *The Silver Saddle*.

Creed exhaled. He did *not* need to deal with this right now. Still, he answered.

"Hey, Luke," Creed said into the phone, greeting the bartender.

"Hey, sorry to bother you. It's your dad again. He's here, and I'm not sure what to do with him. I think he came in drunk, and now he's passed out on the bar. Already fell off his stool twice."

Creed glanced at the clock on the truck dash. It was five minutes after nine in the morning. "Thanks for letting me know. I'll be by in a few minutes." He ended the call and set the phone back on the bench seat.

"Everything okay?" Kat asked.

Creed didn't want to remind Kat of the disaster that was his family, but he also knew that if he left his dad to fend for himself, Rick would end up in jail. Or worse yet, he'd get behind the wheel drunk. Tightened his grip on the steering wheel, he met Kat's eye. Instead of the cold stares she'd been giving him, her eyes held worry.

"Rick's been drinking again," Creed said. He'd always called his dad by his first name. *Dad* never felt appropriate. "Apparently, he's passed out at *The Silver Saddle.*"

Kat was quiet as they passed the third and final block of Main Street. Then she said, "Do you want to go get him?"

It pained Creed that Kat was not shocked by what he'd just told her. She knew enough about Rick that her first instinct was to ask if Creed *wanted* to go pick him up his dad. He also knew she wouldn't judge him if he didn't.

"Yeah, I better." Creed started to turn off Main Street. "I'll drop you off at Eleanor's and come get you when I'm done. It shouldn't take long. I—"

"I'll go with you."

Creed's chest tightened, but he kept his eyes on the road. "You don't have to do that."

"I know," Kat added, quietly. "But you're going to need someone to drive his car."

Creed squeezed the steering wheel again, remembering how many times Kat had helped him with Rick. She'd seen his father passed out, in handcuffs, crazy, belligerent. Even back when they were just kids. He remembered the first time

Kat had driven Rick's truck. She'd had her driver's license for exactly one week. Jesse, Kat, and Creed were driving home from a high school football game, high on life, when they found Rick stumbling around on the road. He'd abandoned his truck in the ditch and was walking to who knows where. That time, Rick hadn't hit anything, so Jesse and Creed manhandled Rick into Creed's truck and got him home. Kat followed behind, driving Rick's truck. That night Creed didn't sleep. He stayed with Rick, trying to keep his father from choking on his own puke.

"He was doing good for a while," Creed said. "Was sober for about six months." Which was the longest Creed had ever seen his father sober.

Kat stayed quiet, and Creed made a U-turn. He got back on Main Street and headed just out of town to where *The Silver Saddle* was nestled in a cradle of trees. There were a handful of cars in the gravel parking lot. The bar-and-grill was known for their weekend breakfast buffet and their Friday night fish fry. That's what most people came for. Not Rick. Rick came for breakfast cocktails.

Creed parked and got out of his truck. Kat got out as well. He couldn't look her in the eye as they entered the restaurant.

Inside, tables and booths were full of families and couples eating pancakes and sipping coffee. Creed made a sharp left and headed toward the bar, where Luke greeted him with a sympathetic look. He was adding a celery stick to a Bloody Mary.

Rick was exactly where Luke had said he was—on a barstool, hunched over on the counter, sleeping. At least he wasn't on the floor.

Luke nodded his head toward Rick. "I didn't serve him. Tried to get him to drink some water, but he basically came in here and crashed."

"Sorry about that," Creed said. "I'll get him out of here."

Creed walked to the end of the bar and placed his hand on his dad's back. He gave him a shake. "Wake up, Rick. Let's go."

Rick's eyes fluttered. He had on a knit hat and the thick flannel jacket he never seemed to be without. He'd be sixty-five this year, and Creed wondered if he'd ever get it together.

"What?" Rick asked, annoyed that he had to open his eyes. Pulling his head up from the bar, he wiped drool off his mouth with his sleeve. "I'm just resting my eyes." His words slurred as he looked at Creed.

"Not anymore. Time to go home." Creed put a hand under Rick's arm to help him off the stool. Rick jerked away but stopped when he saw Kat.

"Kat?" Rick squinted like he was having a hard time seeing.

"Hi, Mr. Sheridan," Kat replied with all the manners Rick didn't deserve. "How about you come with us? We'll get you home."

"What you doing here?" Rick raised his arms like he was going to give Kat a hug. Creed tightened his grip on his dad's arm. He certainly wasn't going to let Rick stumble and cling to Kat, not in this state. Rick sneered at Creed. "I thought you left this guy forever ago." His comment was for Kat, but he was looking at Creed. The only reason it hurt was because Kat had heard it.

"Come on," Creed pushed his arm around Rick's back to haul him off the stool.

Rick stood and sighed, like he was giving in. "I'm tired. Need a nap."

Creed started walking Rick away from the bar. He gave a wave to Luke, who waved back before putting two Bloody Mary drinks on a tray. Just then, the kitchen door swung open and Zoey came out. She grabbed the drink tray from the bar but set it down when her eyes landed on Creed. Her blonde hair was pulled back in a ponytail, and her smoky-shadowed eyes widened.

Zoey walked toward Creed, stuffing her notepad and pen in the black apron that hung around her waist. "You need some help?" She slowed when she noticed Kat.

"It's okay, Zoey. Got it handled. Thanks." Creed wanted to get out of the bar before Rick made a scene that might scar the unsuspecting families just trying to enjoy their pancakes and coffee. Plus, he saw Zoey zoning in on Kat.

Zoey wasn't Creed's girlfriend, but they'd been dating for a few months. She was good company and had even gone to a few rodeos with him, but Creed didn't see anything long term with her. And he'd told her that. A few times. She always agreed, saying they could date casually, but Creed knew she was just saying what he wanted to hear. It had been a bad idea to invite her to Joyce and Gene's last night for dinner, but Creed didn't want to be alone when he saw Kat for the first time in years.

"Hey," Zoey said to Kat, sounding uncertain. Kat returned the greeting. Zoey turned back to Creed. "You sure you don't need help? I can take my break early."

"No, I got it," Creed reiterated, and started walking with Rick again, headed toward the door.

Zoey put her hand on Creed's arm. "Call me later?" She looked nervous.

Creed nodded. "Sure." His response received a smile. Zoey dropped her hand and went to retrieve the drinks from the bar.

Kat turned and walked to the door. She held it open for Creed to haul Rick through. She didn't seem bothered—not by his drunk father or the accusing stare Zoey had given her. Kat stayed quiet and helped Creed get Rick into the back seat of his truck.

She truly deserved so much. More than he could ever give her.

CHAPTER FOUR

Kat drove Rick's truck from *The Silver Saddle* to the trailer where Rick lived, though Creed wouldn't let her help him get Rick inside. Instead, she sat in the cab of Rick's truck, staring at the trailer Creed had grown up in. Kat did *not* think fondly of the dark and dreary rectangular house. She'd never seen Creed happy there. She'd seen him happy plenty of other places, but never there. Even now, as a grown man, he was still dealing with his father's antics. She hated that for him.

When worry overtook her patience, Kat opened the truck door, ready to go into the trailer and see what was taking so long. She stopped when Creed finally came out. His jaw was tight, and he wiped a hand over his face as he walked toward her.

"Would you mind driving Rick's truck back to your parent's place?" Creed asked. "If he's back to drinking, I'm not giving him the option of driving."

"Of course." She sat back down in the driver's seat.

"Thanks." Creed turned toward his truck. "Meet you at Eleanor's first?"

Kat gave him a nod and started up Rick's truck. She followed Creed to the sewing shop, which was a few blocks off Main Street. Eleanor was Joyce's age and had a shop set up in the mother-in-law suite above her garage. She'd known Kat and Creed since they were kids, so once they arrived, their time in the shop was filled with small talk and chatter, mostly on Eleanor's part. It was nice to have her fill the uneasy gap between Kat and Creed.

Kat went first, heading into the dressing room to shimmy into her bridesmaid dress. It fit perfectly, and it was obvious that Hazel had great taste. The dresses she'd picked out were emerald green, tied at the neck, cinched at the waist, and fell to the ankle. However, even though she loved the dress, Kat was not about to leave the dressing room. In her rush this morning, she hadn't changed out of her sweaty sports bra or her granny panties. And neither was particularly flattering under the pretty dress. Kat poked her head out and asked Eleanor to join her in the dressing room to check her measurements.

When Kat was back in her jeans and sweater, Creed took his turn. Kat busied herself looking through a photo album which showcased dresses Eleanor had made over the years. However, she couldn't help but peek at Creed when he stepped out of the dressing room in his suit. The slate-gray jacket was buttoned at his waist and served as a spotlight for his wide shoulders and slim waist. His emerald tie matched her bridesmaid dress, but more so, she noticed how it matched his eyes.

After a few poses and Eleanor's approval, Creed turned back to the fitting room and Kat's eyes darted down to the photo album. What was she doing? She gave her head a little shake, knocking out the image of Creed. Giving him a once-over was like playing chicken with a train—an adrenaline rush that never ended well.

After gathering the rest of the bridesmaid dresses, Creed and Kat loaded the full garment bags into Creed's truck and headed back to her parents' house. Kat parked Rick's rusty truck next to the garage and got out, wondering how long Creed would keep the vehicle from his dad.

When she met Creed at the front of his truck, he said, "Sorry. I didn't mean to get you involved in that."

"Don't be sorry. You're not responsible for what your dad does." She handed him Rick's keys, and Creed's fingers slid across her palm. His touch hit her with a familiar jolt, and she quickly released the keys. Creed caught them, and Kat stuffed her hands in her jean pockets.

"I know." Creed spun the keys around a finger. His voice didn't hold his usual confidence.

When Kat was in the bar, she'd wanted to yell at Rick, tell him to shape up or ship out. Creed had been dealt a crappy hand, to put it mildly, when it came to parents. He was just fourteen when the state seized him from his drug addict mother and placed him with his father, who wasn't any better. Creed got into a lot of trouble when he was a kid, but Kat didn't blame him. He didn't have anyone to look out for him. Not until he got caught for underage drinking and ended up doing community service. The judge sentenced him to six months of shoveling horse manure before school—at the Weston barn.

Kat remembered the first time she had seen Creed. He was scowling and mumbling as he cleaned his first horse stall. And he was doing a crappy job. He wasn't taking the time to properly sift through the bedding and remove every piece of manure.

"Dad's going to make you clean that stall again," she'd said, as Creed rolled the wheelbarrow to the next stall. Fourteen-year-old Creed had told her to shut up. It was the first thing he'd ever said to Kat. Twelve-year-old Kat would've popped him in the nose if he wasn't twice her size. Instead, she told her brothers, and a scuffle proceeded in the barn aisle.

Creed ended up having to clean that stall again. Kat and her brothers were grounded for a week.

But Gene and Joyce kept on Creed, holding him to his tasks. They started inviting him to supper and eventually hired him, after his community service was done, to continue helping around the barn. That wasn't the end of Creed's troubles, but it was the beginning of a real family for him. Soon he was deemed an honorary Weston. He gained two parents, two brothers, and three sisters. Then, years later—after Kat's senior year—he became her first love.

Creed pulled Kat out of the past when he said, "He was actually clean for six months. Longest I've seen him sober. He was even going to AA meetings with me."

Kat knew how hard it had been for Creed to go to his first AA meeting, but he'd been sober for six years now. Rick should follow his son's example. "I hope he wises up and starts going to meetings again."

"Me too." Creed sighed like he was done with the conversation. He opened his truck door and grabbed the bagged, hanging dresses. "Where do you want me to put these?"

"I can take them." She took the dress bags from Creed, letting them fold over her arm. "Mom told me to hang them up in her room."

"Oh, before I forget—" Creed dug back into his truck. "Here are your keys. Evan and I got your rental car this morning. We had to pull it out of the field, but it started right up. Tougher than I thought it would be. I parked it back by the barn."

Kat's mouth popped open. They had done all that before he'd even gotten to her parents' place this morning? "Oh, *thank you.*"

Creed handed her the key and hopped back in his truck. "See ya later, Kat," he said before shutting his door.

Kat wasn't sure why she was surprised by what Creed had done. He'd always taken care of her. He may not have always made the right choices, but his heart was in the right place. All but that one time.

Kat spent the rest of the afternoon working on reports for her boss. She holed herself up in the boys' bedroom, away from the commotion downstairs. But even with the bedroom door shut, she heard chatter and laughing. Kat wanted to be with her family. She also wanted to keep her job *and* get the promotion she was aiming for. She was having an ugly tug-of-war game with herself and wasn't sure how much longer she could stare at her computer screen.

When Kat moved to Chicago and started working at the Fortune Five Hundred company *Genius Appliances*, she knew she'd have to work her tail off. And she did. She started off as a sales assistant and spent every waking minute learning the business, pushing herself, and surpassing goals the company set for her. After a year, she was promoted to an account manager and had since been building her sales territory, doubling her accounts each year. Now, she was after her boss's position as national sales manager. Wendy was transferring to the company's international division next month, and her position needed to be filled. Kat had completed three interviews, including a grueling session in front of the board. She would find out next week if she got the job. And a recommendation from Wendy would give Kat the edge over her competition.

So these reports needed to be perfect.

Kat sat cross-legged on the bed and stared at her laptop, which was propped up on a pillow. She might go cross-eyed if she stared at spreadsheets or sales reports for one more minute. Exhausted, she toppled over and grunted into the quilt. Just then her laptop rang, like a phone.

"Oh no." Kat cringed and sat up, figuring Wendy was checking up via another video call. But when she looked at the screen, she was relieved to see the call was from her coworker Lei.

Kat clicked the *accept* button on the screen.

Lei's face filled the screen, and Kat immediately relaxed.

"Kat!" Lei whisper-shouted. She pushed her trendy red cat-eye glasses up on her nose. "When are you getting your new phone? I can't handle you being out of the office *and* not being able to talk to you. I need my work-wife back!" Lei looked at her expectantly. They both broke into smiles.

"I miss you too," Kat said. "I get back Sunday night, so I expect to see you at Happy Hour at five o'clock sharp on Monday."

"You know it," Lei replied like that wasn't even a question.

Lei was a product engineer and had started at *Genius Appliances* a few years ago. She and Kat had worked together on a computerized toaster project that never came to fruition. Instead, an immediate friendship had hatched.

"We're going to need a full-on vent session and at least three margaritas. Wendy is killing me." Kat sighed.

"Work-shmurk." Lei ogled Kat over the top of her eyeglasses. "I want to hear about whoever that hunka-hunka-burning-love was that snuck into our video call this morning. Spill it."

"What? You saw him?" As soon as the words left her mouth, Kat knew she'd just egged Lei on. "I mean, Wendy didn't say anything, so I thought no one else saw him either."

"Uh, I saw him." Lei raised her eyebrows. "And the only reason Wendy didn't see him was because she's too distracted by the sound of her own voice."

Kat chuckled. *So true.* "He's nobody. Just a family friend." Even though Lei and Kat were close, she'd never told Lei about Creed. When Lei and Kat met, Kat was already dating Michael and she'd pushed the memory of Creed to the back of her brain.

Lei pursed her lips. "Yep. Don't believe you. I saw the way he looked you up and down like a popsicle in the desert. He wanted to—"

"Lei!" Kat squeaked, surprised to hear what her friend thought she'd seen.

"I'm just saying," Lei said. "You're a free woman, and that man looked like a snack."

"I'm not ready for snacks," Kat replied. *Especially that one.* It was nice to talk to someone who knew the truth about her broken engagement. Lei had been Kat's confidant and shoulder to cry on through the ups and downs of the past few months. She knew Kat's struggles when it came to Michael.

Lei straightened abruptly. "Oh, no. Boss man is here. Good thing his annoying voice carries. I can hear him coming down the hall. Gotta go." She leaned in close to the camera. "And you better be ready to spill the beans come Monday." Lei winked and ended the call.

Kat smiled. Lei always made her laugh, and she'd really needed a chuckle. Even if her friend was wrong about Creed. If Lei had seen the way he'd kissed Zoey last night, right in front of Kat, she'd think differently.

"Time for a break." Kat closed her laptop, got off the bed, and stretched. It was just after three o'clock. She had a few more hours to finalize her reports before sending them off to Wendy. She had time to go downstairs and take a short break.

Once in the kitchen, Kat found the source of all the chatter and laughter. Hazel and her sister, Frankie, sat at the kitchen table with Anne and Joyce. Mason jars, candles, ribbon, and twine were scattered across the table, along with multiple pairs of scissors and a few hot glue guns.

"Kitty Kat!" Frankie jumped up from her chair and raced across the kitchen to hug Kat. Her red hair bounced around her shoulders.

Kat opened her arms and grabbed Frankie into a tight hug. "Little Miss Frankie. How come you weren't here for dinner last night?" Like Creed, Frankie had been honorably inducted into the Weston family. Frankie's mom, Rose, was Joyce's best friend, before she passed a few years ago. Frankie had always felt like a cousin, even though they weren't related.

"Had a puking kid and a sick horse." Frankie wrinkled her freckled nose at Kat. "But all is better now, so I came to help with the table decorations."

"Good to see you." Kat squeezed Frankie's arms.

Frankie smiled. "You too."

"Do you guys need one more to help?" Kat asked the table of women. "I might not be handy with a sewing machine or an oven, but I'm pretty decent with a hot glue gun."

The table chuckled.

"Come on," Joyce said over her shoulder. "And grab a mug. I've got cider in the crockpot."

Kat licked her lips, almost drooling at the mention of her mom's mulled cider. She looked forward to the cider every fall, but had missed out on sipping the sweet concoction last year when she couldn't get away from work until Christmas.

Kat walked to the crockpot on the kitchen counter and removed the lid. Steam and spices wafted up. Kat breathed them in like her life depended on it. She grabbed a mug from a cabinet and picked up the ladle from the counter. She dipped the ladle deep into the cider, below the cinnamon sticks and orange slices. She filled her mug a bit too full but sipped with every step on her way back to the table.

"Seriously, Mom. How do you make this *so good*?" Kat took a seat between Anne and Joyce.

"I gave you the recipe." Joyce was tying a bow of burlap around a mason jar. "Hand me the hot glue gun."

Kat passed the hot glue gun to her mom. "I tried making it, but it didn't turn out the same," Kat said.

Last fall, on a day when Kat was especially missing her family, she'd called her mom and asked for the cider recipe. Then she'd scoured her local market for each ingredient and threw it all together, only to be disappointed when she took her first sip. "It tasted kind of bland when I made it."

Joyce put a dab of clear glue behind the bow, adhering it to the glass jar. "Did you scour the cinnamon sticks and the ginger? Give a little squeeze to a few of the orange slices?"

Kat tried to remember. "I think so." Maybe she'd skipped over those parts of the recipe? Kat didn't claim to be the cook her mother or sister was. She'd rather eat food than prepare it.

Joyce set down the hot glue gun. "Probably that fancy-dancy crockpot you have, then. Too many buttons. You need one like mine."

Kat grinned. "It does have a lot of buttons." Kat's crockpot was from *Genius Appliances'* premium appliance line. In addition to the slow-cook option, it could sauté, steam, pressure-cook, and self-clean. It looked like a small spaceship, but apparently it wasn't smart enough to make mulled cider.

"Mine has one knob and three settings. Off, low, and high. There's no confusing that. And I've had it since your father and I first got married," Joyce said.

"They don't make things like they used to," Anne said as she cut more burlap ribbon.

Hazel put a white candle in one of the finished jars and set it in the middle of the table. "I agree. I was making mini apple pies the other day for the bed and breakfast, and my food processor broke. I was just trying to cut chilled butter into the flour and the little thing started smoking. I'd only had it a few months."

Anne and Joyce made noises of agreement. Frankie raised her shoulders and looked at Kat like the rest of the ladies were part of some conspiracy theory. Kat smirked back at Frankie. She knew Frankie had about as much talent in the kitchen as she did. Kat only knew what a food processor was because it was part of her product line at work. She'd never actually used one.

Grabbing an empty jar and one of the ribbons Anne had cut, Kat joined the craft session. Soon, ribbon-clad mason jars lined the table.

"Oh, I love them," Hazel said, squeezing her hands together at her chest. "They're going to look so beautiful on the tables at the wedding. Jesse is cutting big slabs of birch to set them on. Thank you all." Her eyes were glassy, and Kat's heart squeezed.

Just then, the sliding door opened and Kat's niece Charlie scooted through. Her blonde curls bounced along with her tutu as she skipped in and jumped on Hazel's lap. "Hey, Momma!"

"Hey, Sweetie." Hazel snatched Charlie up with one arm and planted a big kiss on her cheek. "How was kindergarten?"

Charlie started explaining the book her teacher had read today, telling everyone what the story was about—a cow, a pig, and a farmyard adventure. Her gestures were dramatic, but her words were quickly drowned out like Kat was underwater. All Kat could see was her sister, Sarah.

Charlie—Charlotte—was Sarah's daughter. She had been just a baby when Sarah died. Charlie got Sarah's blonde curls and big personality, and after Sarah passed, Jesse got Charlie. He adopted her and was the best single dad Kat had ever seen. Then Hazel and her daughter, Grace, came along. Now they were a family. A unit. Kat was so unbelievably happy for them, but in that moment, it felt like the loss of Sarah had kicked her in the neck.

Kat cleared her throat and stood from the table. She turned and took her empty mug to the kitchen sink. She didn't want to cry.

"Aunt Kitty Kat?" Charlie called and pattered across the kitchen to take Kat's hand. When Kat was little, *Kitty Kat* was her nickname. Now it was mostly her nieces and nephews who called her that. And Frankie.

Kat swallowed the lump in her throat. "Hey, baby girl." She picked Charlie up and set her on her hip.

"Will you play kickball with us?" Charlie's eyes were the size of saucers.

Kat tickled Charlie's tummy. Charlie giggled. "You know I will." She could play one game of kickball before getting back to work. She *wanted* to. And not just because Anne gave her a hard time about not spending enough time with her nieces and nephews.

Charlie squealed, and when Kat set her down, the little girl took her hand and pulled. "We can play boys against girls!" Charlie said.

Kat followed her outside into the backyard and waved at the group of kids. She did a quick count of boys and girls. If it were just her nieces, nephews, and Frankie's boys, they would've had even teams. But in addition to the kids, it looked like Jesse, Evan, and Creed also wanted to play. Evan and Jesse were dropping bases into place. Creed was bouncing the big, rubber ball in his hands.

Charlie let go of Kat's hand and ran toward her cousins.

"Girls against boys! Girls against boys!" Charlie screamed with her little fists in the air. "We'll kick your booties!" She shook her tutu.

While Kat appreciated her niece's enthusiasm for female power, there was way more testosterone in this backyard than estrogen. "I don't think we have enough players," Kat started to say, but her cousin, Myra, jogged over from the barn. She wore cutoff shorts and cowboy boots. Her long black ponytail swayed behind her.

"Go get your momma and the rest of your aunties," Myra said to Charlie and gave her a shoo with her hand. "We need backup."

Charlie raced off, excitedly yelling before she got into the house.

Myra stopped in front of Kat. "I told Charlie we'd kick these guys' butts just like we did in the old days." She gave a jerk of her thumb toward Jesse, Evan, and Creed. They responded with jeers and cat calls. "You up for it, cous'?"

Kat looked at the boys who now reminded her of a bunch of naughty middle-schoolers on the playground. Had she just fallen back in time?

"Oh, you know it," she said to Myra. They gave each other a high-five.

"Somebody say they needed some women to kick these boys' butts?" Frankie called as she left the back deck. She was tying her red hair into a ponytail as she jogged over. Anne and Hazel were behind her. They didn't have the same zeal as Frankie, but still looked game to play.

Kat gave the rest of the ladies high-fives as they joined her and Myra. Out in the field, Jesse and Creed gave each other a chest bump. Evan stretched out his hamstrings. Frankie's little boys were imitating with chest bumps of their own. Anne's teenagers were smirking like this was surely a joke. Kat chuckled, but her competitive side was bubbling up.

The women and girls huddled.

"Can I go first?" Charlie was hopping around in the middle of the huddle.

"You sure can," Kat said. "You go first and then your sister." Both Charlie and Grace nodded attentively and then scooted off toward home base, ready to kick the ball. Kat gave a knowing look to Frankie and Myra. "We'll lead with cuteness and then bring in the ringers."

Frankie and Myra smirked at Kat, knowing exactly what she meant. Behind them, Anne and Hazel were talking to Anne's two daughters about cookies they planned to make that night.

Myra jerked her head toward the cookie conversation. "We're going to have to make up for the bakers in the back."

Kat and Frankie nodded like they were getting ready to play the Superbowl.

"We can hear you," Anne said in a singsong.

Hazel laughed. "I'm counting on you guys to make up for my complete lack of athleticism."

"First kicker's up!" Jesse yelled from the outfield—which consisted of the grassy area between the house and the barn.

"Ready, Daddy!" Charlie yelled back. She was standing directly on home plate, wiggling her tutu-covered butt. She stared intently at Creed, who had the rubber ball and was trying hard not to laugh at the little girl.

"Here it comes," Creed yelled, and rolled the ball gently toward Charlie. She kicked it with all her might. It bounced about ten feet, and Charlie ran like the dickens. The ball stopped closest to Creed, but he took his time picking it up. Charlie made it to first base, where she proceeded to jump and yell.

Kat cupped her hands around her mouth and yelled with the rest of the women, "Good job, Charlie! Way to go!"

Grace was up next, and it was much the same, only she kicked the ball close to third base. Frankie's oldest son, Tommy, grabbed it. He threw it to Evan, who was manning first base, but Grace got on base before Evan could tag her. More cheering ensued.

"Two on base. Now it's time for the big guns," Kat whispered to Frankie and slapped her on the back.

Frankie ran toward home plate, and Kat watched the field change. Creed's smirk wiped away, and he angled himself like a major league pitcher on the mound. Jesse was in the outfield and said something to the other boys before leaning in, looking ready to run. This time, when Creed rolled the ball, it flew across the ground like it'd been shot, but Frankie met it with her foot and sent the ball soaring into the air. The women screamed as Frankie ran, but the ball went straight for Creed. He jumped, looking like a basketball player even though he was clad in a T-shirt and jeans, and caught it.

"You're out!" Creed yelled as his feet landed back on the ground.

The guys cheered, and Frankie threw her hands up in defeat. As she jogged back, she squinted at Kat and said, "Get 'em, Kitty Kat!"

Kat had on her serious face now. She approached the base, stretched out both hamstrings, and swung her arms like she might fight someone. She was glad she'd changed into her running shorts this afternoon.

"You about done?" Creed called, holding the ball in front of his chest.

Kat held up one finger, telling him to wait. She did a little jog in place and thought she saw Creed smirk. "I'm ready now, smiley. Bring it."

Creed wound up, and the ball shot toward her.

CHAPTER FIVE

Creed tried hard to focus. He couldn't go easy on Kat, but his eyes kept flicking down to her bare legs, especially as she stretched and hopped around. Was she doing that on purpose? Was she trying to distract him? Her antics were on the verge of cheating, and Creed knew she'd do just about anything to win. Kat loved to show the boys what she was made of, and Creed had known a boys-versus-girls game would entice Kat outside. He must've been in the mood to torture himself because he was the one who had suggested the game to Charlie.

But right now, he couldn't focus on his self-destructiveness, or Kat's legs. Which were actually one and the same.

"You about done?" Creed called, wanting to stop Kat's tormenting prancing.

Kat yelled back with all the sass he expected. When she finally stilled, Creed zoned in on home plate, wound up, and let the heat fly. He fired the red rubber ball, and Kat smacked it right back at him.

She knew exactly where to kick it.

Kat aimed to the left, arching the ball out of his reach and over Tommy's head. It bounced into the outfield, and Jesse raced to snatch it from the ground.

"Get it, Jess!" Creed yelled, urging on his friend.

Jesse snatched up the ball and shot it over to first base, but by the time Evan caught it, Kat was already there, jumping on the base much like Charlie had.

Kat was fast. Like a cheetah. A competitive, silly, jumping cheetah.

The girls all cheered. Creed shook his head and then gestured at Kat, letting her know that he was watching her. She stuck her tongue out at him, and he instantly missed her, even though she was right there in front of him. This was the Kat he fell in love with. The carefree, fun-loving, up-for-anything Kat.

"It's time for beast-mode!" Myra yelled. Her overzealous voice snatched Creed's attention back to home plate, and he waved all the guys to step back. Jesse had already moved to the edge of the corn field. Myra was *not* kidding when she warned of her beast-mode. Creed had never met another girl that could kick like she could. Even in jean shorts and cowboy boots, Myra could put a football kicker to shame.

The bases were loaded. If Myra slapped this ball into the corn field, she'd score four runs for the girls.

"Get ready, boys!" Creed called. Then he stepped up, focused, and pitched his best attempt at a curveball. Anything to throw Myra off.

It didn't work. Myra kicked the rubber ball into the air like a cannon and then loped off to first base like she had all the time in the world.

Creed's neck craned as he followed the ball through the blue sky, certain it would land in the corn stalks, but Jesse launched himself into its path and managed to slap it down. Creed hooted as Jesse landed flat on the grass. The ball bounced back into play, and Anne's son Bryce grabbed it. At that point, everyone was shouting and cheering. Charlie had made it to home base, and Grace wasn't far behind. Bryce had quite the arm and launched the ball in, to Creed. When Creed caught it, he saw Kat rounding third and knew she'd beeline it for home.

Spinning, Creed raced toward her.

Creed and Kat locked eyes, both running toward home base. He held tightly to the ball, determined to tag her with it. If he threw it, Kat might dodge it—if her reflexes were as good as they used to be.

Nearing home base, Creed was one step ahead of Kat. He had this in the bag. He'd tag Kat and go after Myra. But as he stepped into the baseline, Creed caught the determination in Kat's eyes and second-guessed his plan.

The ball was in his outstretched left hand, but Kat spun to his right, trying to bypass him. Without thinking, Creed reached for her with his open arm.

She rammed into him. Like a linebacker.

Kat squealed. Creed grunted. And they crashed together in a mess of legs and arms.

Creed ended up on his back. He might've been able to hold on to the ball if Kat hadn't landed on top of him, but when her body smashed against his, he forgot all about the ball. His grip slipped, and the ball rolled away . . . leaving him blanketed by Kat.

They were nose to nose. Chest to chest. Legs entangled. Breath heaving.

Time slowed, and Creed had a strong instinct to wrap his arms around her, even though she was not his. Before he could make the stupid choice to do it anyway, Kat slid off his chest. *Thankfully.* She rolled off Creed and onto her back.

Charlie ran over and looked down at them both.

"Momma said you're not supposed to do that. We aren't playing football." Charlie put her hands on her hips. "You both lose."

Frankie was behind Charlie, barely suppressing a laugh.

Creed laid there, thinking just how right Charlie was.

"Two runs for the girls," Kat said, and got to her feet. She brushed herself off and peered down at Creed, much like Charlie was. "You're not supposed to stand in the baseline."

"You're not supposed to ramrod me like a linebacker," Creed countered.

Frankie laughed. "I think you two just cancelled each other out. You both broke the rules."

Kat gave a dramatic gasp. Then a playful wink. "Okay, fine." She reached her hand out, and Creed took it. As she helped him up, they shared the slightest of smirks. Then she bounded away, over to her teammates, and Creed hoped Kat's smirk was a step in the right direction, that they could go back to how it used to be. At least being friends.

After a rule refresher, the kickball game continued—minus the tackling. The girls won by two runs, and the guys were sour about it until Joyce came out of the house with a pitcher of lemonade.

"Everyone's a winner here," Joyce said, pouring lemonade into plastic cups. Creed took two and thanked Joyce. Then, against everything his brain was shouting, he walked toward Kat. She was on the far side of the barn, leaning on a fence, staring into the pasture.

He walked up behind her, wanting to break the ice. "You on a kickball team in Chicago?"

She turned her head and chuckled. It was what he had been aiming for, and he was pleased. "No. Not sure they know what kickball is in Chicago."

He offered her one of the plastic cups. "Just seems like you've been practicing."

She smiled softly and took the cup. "Thanks." As she took a sip, Creed glanced into the pasture, at the horses grazing, and realized what Kat had been looking at.

"I know he misses you," Creed said, referring to Kat's horse, Diesel. The black-and-white Paint horse had been born in the Westons' barn on Kat's thirteenth birthday. Diesel had been Kat's ever since that day. He was the first horse she'd ever started under saddle on her own and had been her partner at many rodeos. Creed could still picture Kat and Diesel rounding barrels and weaving poles. They were a beautiful team. Surely, she missed him too.

Kat stared into the pasture, silent. Creed couldn't tell what she was thinking.

He placed an arm on the fence. "I bet if you whistle, he'd run right over. He'd know your whistle anywhere."

She looked down at the ground. "I know he's taken care of," she said.

It was a statement, not a question, but an odd one at that. Of course, he was taken care of. Diesel had a permanent place at the Westons' until the day that he died. He wasn't going anywhere, even if Kat wasn't here to ride him like she used to.

Maybe she was worried Diesel wouldn't recognize her? Creed knew Diesel would, but it looked like Kat needed a push.

"I can call him if you'd like." Creed took a breath, preparing to give one of his earsplitting whistles, but Kat grabbed his forearm. He stopped and looked at her.

"I don't want to see him." Her face was slack. Serious. She didn't say anything else. Instead, she turned and walked back to the house, leaving both Creed and Diesel behind.

CHAPTER SIX

The next day, Kat woke well before sunrise, reviewed all her boss's nitpicky notes and made the requested changes to her reports. Then she closed her laptop and spent the rest of the day helping with wedding preparations.

"Where do you want these?" Kat asked Jesse. She and Evan stood at the back of the open horse trailer. It was full of rental furniture which the three of them had retrieved from the *Elks Club*. The tables and chairs would be used for the wedding and reception on Saturday.

"Let's stack them all along the back of the carriage house," Jesse replied.

Kat grabbed two folding chairs from the trailer, one under each arm. Evan and Jesse did the same—but with round tables. As they walked the short distance to the carriage house, Kat remembered all the fun times she'd had here as a kid. The carriage house faced the lake and was walking distance from her parents' place. Kat and her siblings had played countless games of hide-and-seek in the building that used to resemble a weathered barn. There'd been slumber parties in sleeping bags on the wooden floor. They'd scared each other with ghost stories and fished from the dock that still floated under the same willow tree.

The memories warmed her heart. Kat was glad to see the carriage house had received some love and was being enjoyed now, in a different way.

"You guys did an amazing job with the renovations," she said as she propped the chairs against the white siding of the carriage house. Hazel had inherited the building and lakefront property when her mom passed. It had since been fixed up and turned into a beautiful bed and breakfast which Hazel and Jesse ran.

"I was just the worker bee." Jesse set the tables next to the chairs. "Hazel was the mastermind. I just followed orders and did as I was told."

"Smart man," Evan said with a smirk. He set the tables he carried next to the others.

Jesse laughed. "I've learned a few things over the years."

"It'll be the perfect place for your wedding," Kat said, taking another glance at the carriage house before heading back to the trailer to grab more chairs. It was only a building, but it held special memories. Now Jesse and Hazel would create another beautiful memory here with their vows.

After an afternoon of hauling around tables and chairs, Kat headed back to her parents' place, intending to take a shower. However, as soon as she stepped in the kitchen, Joyce called to her from the living room.

"I think your new phone showed up," her mom said from the couch. Dad was in the recliner, his feet kicked up. The six o'clock news played on the TV. Thelma and Louise were curled up in their laps. "It's on the table."

Kat sprang toward the table, excited to connect with the outside world again. For the past few days, she'd felt a little lost without her phone, though it was nice to have the peace and quiet. She opened the box and powered on her new phone, happy to see all her contacts and apps had transferred over. She clicked into her voicemails and scanned through them. There were a handful of work-related messages and a few from her mom, which Kat was sure Joyce had left during Kat's turbulent arrival to Maple Bay. But it was the last few voicemails that grabbed her attention.

At the bottom of the list, there was a voicemail from Michael. And two from Creed.

Kat knew what Creed's messages said. They'd been on her phone for over five years, but she couldn't bring herself to delete them. The oldest was a short message he'd left her when they'd started dating again, as adults. She was just over thirty, between jobs, and had moved back to Maple Bay to save money while she figured out her options. Kat had rented a house in town, and she'd been seeing Creed for a few weeks. He'd called to tell her to turn on the oven, that he'd be over in ten minutes, and he was bringing chocolate chip cookie dough and vanilla ice cream. She vividly remembered that night. They'd baked cookies, laughed about old times, cuddled, kissed, and had fallen asleep in each other's arms. It was the night Kat remembered how deep her love was for him.

She'd listened to that voicemail about a million times.

The second voicemail from Creed was just before she moved to Chicago. It was the opposite of the first, and Kat had only listened to that message once. She couldn't bring herself to hear Creed's voice crack and beg.

Kat closed her eyes. Why couldn't she let those memories go? Why hadn't she deleted Creed's messages?

When she opened her eyes, her finger moved quickly. It landed on Michael's voicemail, and she pressed the phone to her ear.

"Hi, Kat," Michael's voicemail started. "I just wanted to check up on you. Can you call me when you get a chance? Let me know how your week is going? Tell your family hi from me."

Kat's heart twisted like a wrung-out rag. What was wrong with her? Why was she running from Michael yet hanging on to feelings for a man who had destroyed her? Michael was a good guy. He cared about her. Why couldn't she be happy with him?

Kat quickly typed out a text message to Michael.

All is good. Thanks for checking. Having fun. Talk soon.

She set her phone on the table and went upstairs, where she promptly changed into leggings and a lightweight hoodie. She needed to go for a run.

When Kat came back into the living room, her mom said, "Make sure you're back before dark."

Kat nodded. Then she kissed her dogs on their scruffy heads. They were happy as clams, tucked into afghans and snuggling with her parents.

"Weatherman said it's going to dip below freezing tonight," Dad said. "Maybe even see some flurries."

That was the thing about October in Minnesota—the weather changed quickly. Yesterday she'd played kickball in the sunshine. Tonight, they might see snow.

"I won't be gone long," Kat reassured her parents. She just needed to run out her anxiety.

Outside, she did a quick stretch and started jogging. She followed the gravel road into town and turned on to Main Street, where she passed brick buildings and striped awnings at a good clip. Opposite the downtown shops was Maple Leaf Lake. For the most part, Kat kept her eyes on the lake, trying to lose herself in the dark-blue water. She'd always played sports but had never run for the sake of running until she moved to the city. In Chicago, Kat belonged to a gym just down the street from her apartment. She liked to end her days on the treadmill or with a run along Lake Michigan.

It was how she kept herself sane—forcing worries from her brain by focusing on her body.

Her little trick was helping now. As Kat looped back toward the house on a different path that led her along the edge of the lake, her anxiety waned. The dirt path below her feet and the tall oak trees surrounding her soothed her worries, and when the backside of the Weston barn came into view, Kat slowed to a walk, intending to start her cooldown routine.

Until a male voice yelled from somewhere up ahead in the woods. "Sasquatch?"

Kat jumped. *What?* Why was someone calling for Bigfoot?

Just then, a fluffy orange cat ran across the dirt path like it was chasing something. Kat jogged ahead and spotted the cat as it bounded toward the lake and onto a wooden dock. A rectangular houseboat was tied to the dock, and the cat trotted toward it, meowing.

Creed stood on the front deck of the houseboat. He waved, looking a bit surprised to see her. "Hey."

The cat jumped from the dock onto the houseboat deck. He rubbed his orange head on Creed's leg and then trotted inside through an open door.

Kat gave a wave. "You have a cat?" That surprised her more than realizing Creed lived on a houseboat. He liked to live in things that were movable or easily left behind—horse trailers, mobile homes, rental houses. But Creed had never been a cat person.

He gave her an awkward grin. "Yeah, but he's not a normal cat. He's cool. More like a dog."

Kat huffed and saw her breath in the cold air. Now that she was standing still, her wet, sweaty clothes were starting to chill her. "His name is Sasquatch?" She crossed her arms over her chest, warding off the cold.

"He was a stray. Kept appearing out of the woods when I was cooking supper." Creed raised a shoulder. "He was skinny, and I started to feed him. Guess he took a liking to me."

Kat smiled. *How sweet.*

"Do you want to come in?" Creed asked. "You look cold."

She shook her head. "Nah, I'm going to get back to the house." She didn't need to be alone with Creed in a small space. She'd just gone for a run to force him out of her head.

A loud beeping came from the houseboat. Creed looked surprised and ran inside just as smoke billowed out his open door.

"Creed?" she called. Kat couldn't see what was happening, but it didn't sound good, so she ran to the lake, across the dock, and jumped aboard the boat. She scooted across the deck and in the door. "You okay?"

Inside, Creed stood in a small kitchen. Smoke poured out an open oven, and he was waving an oven mitt at the beeping fire alarm on the ceiling.

"Can you open that window?" He pointed behind her. "Forgot I turned the oven to broil."

Kat turned and pushed open the big window next to the door. Creed opened another window over the sink. He continued waving the oven mitt at the alarm, and Kat joined him, finding a paper plate on the kitchen counter. They waved and coughed, and the smoke eventually started to clear.

When the fire alarm finally stopped beeping, Creed set the oven mitt down on the counter. "It's a good thing I'm well stocked on frozen pizza." He pulled a pan from the oven and set it in the sink. The pizza was charred. Black.

"Yikes. That's definitely well done." Kat made a face and set the paper plate back where she'd found it.

Creed shook his head, and Sasquatch appeared from under the two-person kitchen table. The cat curled around Creed's legs. He meowed like nothing strange had just happened.

"I'm glad *you* enjoyed your dinner," Creed said.

Sasquatch meowed again, and Kat grinned. She looked around. Minus the smoke, the inside of the houseboat was cute. Beautiful wood cabinets and miniature appliances filled the right wall. A small table and cushy couch lined the other. A cast-iron woodstove glowed in the corner, and the far end of the boat looked like it led to a bedroom.

"Welcome to my place." Creed tried scraping the pizza from the pan with the pizza cutter and quickly gave up.

"How long have you lived here?"

"A few years."

"It's nice," Kat said, knowing Creed wasn't known for setting down roots. He'd spent much of his twenties going from rodeo to rodeo. She was surprised he'd finally made a home, even if it was movable. She touched the well-crafted cabinets. "These are beautiful."

"Thanks," he said. "I made them."

Kat shot him a look. "*You* made these?" Creed had always been handy, but she'd never known him to make anything like this.

He nodded. "The table and chairs too. They're all made from reclaimed barn wood."

"Wow." She looked the furniture over, genuinely impressed. "This is nicer than stuff I've seen at high-end boutiques in Chicago. Seriously. Where'd you learn to do that?"

"A buddy of mine taught me some woodworking basics when I was laid up. I started playing around from there."

"After you broke your leg?" Kat had heard all about it from her family. The year after she'd moved to the city, Creed had gotten hung up on a bronc and smashed between the flailing horse and some metal panels. His leg broke in three places. He was lucky it hadn't been worse.

Creed ran a hand through his sun-kissed blond hair. "Yeah, I was going crazy not being able to rodeo. I needed something to keep me busy. Was lucky I found this." He ran his fingers along the edge of a cabinet. "I almost fell back into drinking. That was a tough year."

Kat knew what he meant. It had been a tough year for her too. "I'm glad you didn't." She felt awkward standing in the middle of his kitchen. "Start drinking again, I mean."

"Me too." He was looking at her intensely. Too intensely. She felt his words before they came out of his mouth and wished she'd already left.

"I think I better go," she said, trying to stall him.

It didn't work.

"I didn't kiss her, Kat. I know in the grand scheme of things, it's not much, but I need you to know that. I need you to understand that."

She shook her head. "I can't do this."

Creed was right. In the grand scheme of things, it wasn't important that he'd kissed Sarah. Or not kissed her. It only mattered that Sarah had died.

"We can't change that night, and I can't keep reliving it," Kat added. Then she turned and walked out the door, hurrying into the night.

CHAPTER SEVEN

"Kat, stop." Creed followed her onto the dock. It wasn't like he hadn't said those words to her before. He had. But she'd never accepted them. "I can't change that night. I wish I could. I've played it over and over in my head, thinking of all the ways I could've—"

Kat spun on her heels and faced him. "You kissed her," she said. "I watched you. And then I ran off like a pouting child. Sarah came after me. Not you. She tried to talk to me, and I wasn't having it. I said horrible things to her that night." Her voice broke. It was like a shard of glass jamming into Creed's chest. "She rode off on Diesel, and the next time I saw her, she was lying on the ground. *Dead.*"

The shard of glass dug in deeper.

Creed had so much he wanted to say. When he knew Kat would be home for Jesse's wedding, all he could think of was how he'd apologize to her. But now, looking at her, seeing how much she hurt, Creed knew there was no apology that would make this better. Sarah's death was not something either of them would get past.

He stood there, frozen, his hands out, wanting to catch her. He wanted to take away her pain. He deserved to carry it. Not her.

Creed's phone rang. It was in his back pocket, and he would've ignored it, but it was Jesse's ringtone. Jesse and Hazel were supposed to be on their way to Duluth to pick up Hazel's grandparents from the airport. Why would he be calling?

"It's Jesse," Creed explained, pulling the phone from his pocket. He answered the call.

"Hey, Creed," Jesse said. "Hazel, Grace, and I are at the hospital in Grand Rapids."

"You're what? At the hospital?" Creed watched as Kat's eyes widened.

"What?" Kat's question was urgent. She stepped toward him. "What happened?"

"I'm putting you on speaker." Creed pulled the phone from his ear and pressed a button. "Kat's here with me."

"Hey, Kat," Jesse started, his voice streaming out of the phone held between them. "I don't want you guys to worry. We're okay, but a car sideswiped us on our way through Grand Rapids. The roads are slick. No one is hurt, but I want to get Hazel checked over just to be sure. I didn't want to tell you guys like this, but Hazel's pregnant. She's not very far along, and we need to make sure the baby is okay."

"Oh my God." Kat's mouth hung open. "What can we do? How can we help?"

"Can you go get Charlie? She's at dance class until seven-thirty. Mom and Dad were going to watch her tonight, but they want to come to the hospital. Evan is going to drive them. I don't know how long this will take."

"Of course," Kat said. "We'll take care of Charlie. Don't worry about her. Just make sure Hazel is okay."

"Thanks," Jesse said. "Creed knows where her class is. Call me if you have any questions. Love you guys." He hung up before Kat or Creed could respond.

Creed shoved the phone back in his pocket. Kat had gone white. Creed put his hands on her arms, and she jerked out of her trance. "Everyone is okay," he said. "I'll grab us jackets, and we can take my truck. It's parked just on the other side of the trail."

Kat nodded. Creed quickly stepped inside his houseboat and grabbed two coats that hung on hooks near the door. Back on the dock, he handed one to Kat. She took it but draped it over one arm instead of putting it on. He led her to his truck, which was parked on a dead-end road across from the dock. The truck roared to life, and Creed wished he'd had time to warm it up. The temperature must've dropped twenty degrees in the last few hours. Kat was shivering as she reached for the seat belt.

"Here, put this on." Creed picked up the coat Kat had dropped onto the seat. He opened it for her to slide into. "You're freezing."

She pressed her lips together but let go of the seatbelt to put an arm in Creed's well-worn Carhartt. He shimmied it over her shoulders, and Kat pulled the coat tight around her. It dwarfed her, looking like a canvas blanket.

"There's gloves in the pockets." Creed put the truck in gear and started down the gravel road, away from the lake. "My truck may be old, but she warms up fast. We'll have heat in no time."

"You know where you're going?" Kat asked. His coat's fleece collar brushed her jaw.

Creed nodded. "Charlie's been taking ballet once a week since this summer. She's at *Tip Toes Dance Studio* over by McDonald's."

Kat swallowed and pulled his coat tighter around her. As tight as it could go. He could see her breath, and Creed was glad warm air was starting to blow out of the dash vents.

"I didn't know they were trying to get pregnant," Kat said.

Creed was careful with his answer. Jesse had told Creed that he and Hazel were ready to add a child to their family, but he'd obviously not said anything to his sister. "I knew they wanted to."

"I hope the baby's okay," Kat said quietly.

"Everyone will be okay." Creed didn't know that for sure, but he wanted to reassure Kat. No sense in getting upset before they knew what was happening.

She nodded, and they drove the rest of the way in silence.

They got to *Tip Toes* about ten minutes before the end of dance class. Creed stepped into the bright studio and held the door open for Kat. They walked in and joined a line of parents who were sitting on plastic chairs along the wall. Charlie was in the middle of the open room, twirling with about ten other girls. When she saw Creed and Kat in the mirrors, she waved excitedly before twirling again.

Creed and Kat sat down next to each other and watched as Charlie finished the routine the class was working on for their first recital. Creed had heard Charlie talk about it a million times. She was excited to dance on stage next weekend. She might've been more excited for the recital than the wedding.

The tension in Kat's body started to ease. "She is so adorable."

Creed smiled. "She knows it, too."

When the class was over, Charlie grabbed her pink, puffy coat and skipped over to Creed and Kat. "Where's Grandma?" she asked.

"Grandma had some stuff to get done, so Creed and I are going to hang out with you tonight," Kat said, as she helped Charlie zip her coat. "How's that sound?"

Charlie raised her white-blonde eyebrows. "We going to eat ice cream and stay up late?"

Creed chuckled. "You know you're supposed to be in bed by nine o'clock. And that's stretching it." Charlie gave Creed a pout. "But I'm sure we can have some ice cream."

Charlie smiled. "Let's go!" She grabbed Creed's and Kat's hands and pulled them out of the studio.

Creed drove the three of them to Jesse and Hazel's house. It was on the lake, next door to *The Carriage House Bed and Breakfast.*

Once they were inside, Creed headed into the kitchen. "How about Auntie helps you get your pajamas on and I'll get us some ice cream?"

"Okay!" Charlie grabbed Kat's hand. Kat barely had time to take off the Carhartt jacket. "Let's go, Aunt Kitty Kat!" Kat followed along, no questions asked. Blue, Jesse's border collie, padded upstairs after them.

Creed scooped up three bowls of strawberry ice cream and started a fire in the brick fireplace. By the time Charlie and Kat came back into the living room, the fire was crackling. Charlie sported her unicorn footie pajamas and ran straight for the coffee table, which held the bowls of ice cream.

"Thank you!" Charlie said, scooping her spoon into the pink treat.

Creed handed a bowl to Kat, and she joined him on the couch, giving him a soft smile. He returned it.

Charlie swallowed a big bite of ice cream and set her bowl on the coffee table. "Can we play Chinese checkers?"

Creed glanced at the clock on the mantel. "One game and then it's time for bed."

Charlie raced off and grabbed a flat box from a basket in the corner of the living room. As she set up the board game on the coffee table, she asked, "Which color you want to be, Aunt Kitty Kat?" Charlie gingerly placed marbles in their slots on the star-shaped board.

Kat scooted to the edge of the couch. "How about green?"

Charlie nodded. "Creed can be blue. I'll be white. Okay?"

"Sounds good to me." Creed moved over on the couch, close to Kat so he could reach the marbles. Charlie knelt on the floor and leaned on the coffee table. The three of them started a game, but Charlie was fading quickly, deflating like a balloon. Each time the little girl moved a marble, she inched down further until her head rested on the table. She only made it through half her ice cream.

When Charlie's eyes started fluttering, Kat whispered to Creed, "I think someone's tired."

Creed rose. "I'll put her to bed." He scooped the little girl into his arms.

Kat stood and kissed Charlie on her forehead. "Good night, sweet girl. Love you."

"Love you," Charlie whispered, her eyes closing.

Charlie was sleeping by the time Creed made it upstairs. He tucked her into bed and turned on her night-light before stepping out. Blue curled up at the foot of her bed like a guardian.

As Creed started down the stairs, he considered what he'd say to Kat. He didn't think it was a good idea to continue their conversation from earlier, especially with what had happened tonight. But now that he'd opened that wound, was there anything else they could talk about? He thought it best to let Kat speak first, let her direct the conversation. But when Creed entered the living room, Kat was sitting on the couch, exactly where he'd left her, staring at the board game like it had hypnotized her.

He stopped, concerned. "Kat?"

She looked up at him. Her eyes were glassy. A tear slipped over her cheek. She hid her face in her hands. By the time he got to her, she was sobbing.

Creed sat down next to her, wrapped an arm around her back, and drew her to him. She weakly resisted. He didn't let go. After a few beats, she curled into him. Kat placed her head under his chin and Creed wrapped both arms around her. He pulled her onto his lap and eased them both back into the couch.

He closed his eyes, feeling helpless as she wept. Her shoulders shook, her pain apparent, and Creed didn't know what to say to make it better. He simply held her. He pressed

Kat to his chest, keeping her safe with his arms. His insides ripped as she cried.

Time escaped him, but eventually Kat's sobs waned to quiet tears. Creed rubbed her back, waiting for her to speak. He'd hold her until she told him not to.

"Everything here reminds me of her," she whispered, and Creed swallowed. "It's so hard. Her being gone. I don't think it's ever going to get easier. I miss her so much."

"I'm so sorry, Kat." He gripped the back of her shirt, wanting to go back in time and make everything right.

Kat sniffled and laid a hand on his chest. "When I heard Jesse say they'd been in a car accident, I imagined the worst." Her fingers curled into a loose fist. "I'm *terrified* of losing someone else I love. I can't lose anyone else."

Creed placed his cheek against the top of her head and let it rest there. They breathed in and out together. "I know." It was the only thing he could say.

Creed knew how hard it was to lose a loved one. They'd lost Sarah. Then he lost Kat. After Sarah passed, Creed thought for sure he'd lose the entire Weston family—the only real family he'd ever had. They'd taken him in when no one else cared. Creed would take a bullet for any of them. That's why it killed him every single day that Kat thought he would do something to intentionally hurt her or Sarah. He hadn't intended for that awful night to go as it had. And he hoped Kat would let him explain—someday. Most of all, he wished he could stop her from hurting.

CHAPTER EIGHT

Kat had held it together. Until Chinese checkers. Playing the board game with Charlie reminded her of all the evenings she and Sarah had played together as kids. When Creed left her alone with the star-shaped board and marbles, feelings she'd forced away came rushing back.

She'd cried, and Creed had pulled her to him. She knew she shouldn't have, but she let herself lean on him, because he understood. She didn't have to explain her grief to Creed. She didn't have to tell him about her sister. He knew. He'd grown up with Sarah, too. He'd been with Kat when Sarah died. There was ease in his familiarity . . . in his strong arms, steady chest, the way he smelled of fresh pine and spiced cinnamon. He made her feel safe. Just as she remembered.

Kat cried until her insides were empty. When she didn't have any tears left, she whispered, "I miss her so much." His shirt was wet against her cheek.

When he tightened his arms around her, Kat closed her eyes, and for a minute, she let herself remember Sarah. Her sister's big smile. The way Sarah could make anyone laugh. How she lived life at her own speed—which was pedal-to-the-metal. Kat wanted to remember the good things, always. It was just that her bad memories were stronger. They were the memories that haunted her, that kept her up at night.

The fight she and Sarah had had that night should never have happened. Kat should've walked away. She should've turned the other cheek. Had Sarah kissed Creed? Yes. Kat saw it with her own eyes. But Sarah was drunk. Kat should've put her sister to bed and talked to her about it in the morning. That was the thing about Sarah. She was impulsive. It was her greatest fault and strength, wrapped into one.

Before their fight, Kat had been at a rodeo with Creed and Jesse. It had been a successful event for all three of them. When they got home, they celebrated with a bonfire on the lake shore, behind the Weston barn. A handful of friends had joined them, but as the clock crept close to midnight, the group dwindled down to Jesse, Creed, Sarah, and Kat.

"Meet me in the barn in ten minutes?" Kat had asked Creed. They were cuddled up next to the campfire. He smiled, and Kat squeezed his hand before running off to saddle Diesel. She and Creed had reconnected romantically and had been dating for about a month, but Kat wanted to make their relationship official. She thought they could take a midnight ride together on Diesel, like they used to when they were teenagers. She'd tell Creed how she'd never fallen out of love with him and hoped she'd hear the same back.

But when Creed didn't show up like he said he would, she left Diesel saddled in the barn and walked outside to look for him. She took a few steps out the backside of the barn and spotted two dark shadows. Creed was walking toward the barn. He had an arm around Sarah. Sarah stumbled, and they both stopped. It looked like Creed was holding Sarah up, and Kat started walking toward them, knowing it was time to put her sister to bed. Sarah had had way too much to drink. She'd had a few rough weeks, and Kat understood why her sister was letting loose. She had a new baby. She should've been happy, but Charlie's father didn't want to be a dad. He'd left town, leaving Sarah and his new baby behind.

Sarah was tipsy and upset, but that didn't excuse what happened next. When Sarah stumbled, Creed caught her, and Sarah reached up and kissed him. She wrapped her arms around his neck and pressed her lips to his. The full moon highlighted their kiss, and Kat thought she heard her own heart rip in two. A sound must've escaped Kat's mouth because both Sarah and Creed turned toward her.

Kat was stunned. Shocked. Wounded.

She backpedaled into the barn. Sarah ran after her, saying she was sorry. But all Kat understood was betrayal, and her hurt bubbled out in the form of words. She called her sister a slut, told Sarah she didn't want to hear excuses. Then Kat stepped into the feed room and locked the door, shutting Sarah out. That was the last time she ever spoke to her sister, because as Kat gathered her thoughts and calmed herself down, Sarah climbed aboard Diesel and galloped off into the night—drunk and distraught.

Kat, Creed, and Jesse had frantically searched for Sarah when they realized she was missing, but Kat had been the one to find her . . . lying in a heap on the road just in front of the house. There were hoof marks scraped across the gravel. Kat guessed that Diesel had slipped and Sarah had fallen. Long after the ambulance came and Kat had endured the wails from her parents and siblings, they learned that Sarah had broken her neck in the fall. She'd died instantly.

Kat couldn't forgive herself.

She could forgive a kiss. A drunken mistake. But she couldn't forgive herself for lashing out at her sister. Sarah was hurting. Kat knew that, but she'd only thought of herself in that moment.

The emotions Kat had experienced tonight, curled up next to Creed, were emotions she'd been fighting for five years. She didn't feel right grieving. She couldn't feel sorry for herself. Not when she'd destroyed her family and hurt every single person she loved.

Including Creed.

"I know you didn't mean to kiss her," Kat spoke into Creed's chest. He stopped breathing, and she lifted her head to look him in the eye. Her cheeks were wet, her heart heavy.

Creed's emerald eyes looked like they carried as much weight as her heart did. "I was trying to get her to the house." He brushed a wet strand of hair from Kat's face. "I didn't realize what she was doing. Otherwise I wouldn't have let it happen."

Kat swallowed. She looked down.

Creed continued. "I tried to stop her from leaving on Diesel."

Kat clenched her eyes shut, remembering the panicked sound of Creed's voice as he screamed for Kat and pounded on the feed room door.

"I know," she said, and that was as much as Kat could take in one day. Wanting to quiet the painful flashbacks, Kat laid her head on Creed's shoulder. She closed her eyes and listened to him breathe. At some point, she slipped into sleep.

Kat woke to the sound of hinges creaking. She opened her eyes, feeling like they'd been rubbed with sandpaper. It was dark. The middle of the night. She was snuggled into a couch, wrapped in an afghan, and confused about where she was until a lamp flicked on. Light illuminated the living room. Jesse's living room. Then Kat remembered the events of the night before.

The car accident. Picking up Charlie. Crying on Creed's shoulder. Falling asleep in his arms.

But now she was alone on the couch. Creed was stretched out on a recliner.

"We're home," Jesse's voice jolted Kat out of her stupor.

"Jesse?" Kat threw the afghan back. She jumped off the couch, realizing that Jesse, Hazel, and Grace had just walked through the front door. She ran to her brother, grabbing him into a hug. "Are you all okay?" She let go and proceeded to hug Hazel and Grace.

"We are," Hazel replied and added a big sigh. "Just shook up and tired."

Kat glanced at Hazel's belly. There was no sign of a baby bump.

"Everyone?" Kat looked back into Hazel's eyes, pleadingly.

"The baby is okay too." Hazel placed a hand on her stomach.

Kat let her shoulders hang in relief. "Thank the Lord. We were so worried."

"Glad everyone is okay," Creed added. He now stood beside Kat. His blond hair looked like he'd run his hand through it one too many times. Kat didn't want to imagine what her face looked like after crying her eyes out.

"I'm so glad you're all safe." Kat gave them each another hug. "And I'm so happy for you guys." She pulled back from hugging Jesse. Blue was now winding between them, fighting Kat for his family's attention. "A baby?"

Jesse smiled. His blue eyes twinkled, even after all they'd been through tonight. "Mom and Dad knew, but we haven't told anyone else."

"I knew," Grace said from her position on the floor where she was scratching Blue's belly.

"But Grace is a world-class secret-keeper," Jesse said. Grace smiled at Jesse.

Hazel ran a hand over her daughter's ponytail. Her other hand was still on her belly. "We're going to announce the news at the wedding. And we're going to tell Charlie the night before."

Grace stood and leaned against her mom. "Charlie can keep a secret, but not for *that* long." Hazel wrapped an arm around Grace's shoulders and gave her a little smirk.

"Congratulations," Creed said. "We'll keep your secret."

"Our lips are sealed." Kat ran two fingers over her mouth like she was zipping it shut.

"Thank you for taking care of Charlie tonight," Hazel said. "Joyce and Gene were so worried. They really wanted to come to the hospital."

"Anytime," Kat and Creed replied at the same time. Then Kat felt silly. Creed lived here. He could step in to help Jesse and Hazel whenever they needed it. Kat lived in another state. She couldn't help at the drop of a hat. If she'd been in

Chicago tonight, she wouldn't have been able to do anything except check in by phone.

"I'm really tired, sweetie," Hazel said to Jesse. "I'm going to check on Charlie and get into bed."

"Of course. Go get snuggled up in bed." Jesse kissed Hazel on the forehead. She said goodnight, giving Kat and Creed each a squeeze on the arm. Grace and Blue followed Hazel upstairs.

"I should really get going too," Kat said. "Should check on Thelma and Louise."

Jesse shook his head. "You know Mom and Dad already have those two pups curled up in bed with them."

Kat did know that. "You should go to bed though," she said to her brother. "You've had a long night."

"Which is why I don't think I can sleep yet." Jesse walked into the kitchen. "You two want to join me for a drink? I'll make hot chocolate."

"Sure." Kat looked at Creed, unsure what she'd find in his face after the night they'd shared.

"I'm going to get going," Creed said, looking uncomfortable. It wasn't what Kat was hoping for.

"You sure?" Jesse asked, opening a cupboard. "I've got marshmallows."

"I'm tired, and I think you guys need some brother-sister time." He walked over to Jesse and gave him a solid hug. "Congratulations, man. That's amazing news. So happy for you guys." They patted each other on the back. "I'll see you guys tomorrow."

Jesse gave his friend one more pat on the back. "Drive safe, please. I know you're not going far, but the roads are slick."

Creed nodded and headed for the door. He gave Kat a tight smile as a goodbye. She found herself wishing that he'd stayed.

"How many marshmallows do you want?" Jesse asked Kat.

She pulled her gaze away from the closed door and looked at her brother. "What?"

"Marshmallows?" Jesse quirked an eyebrow as he filled the teapot with water.

"Oh." Kat stepped into the kitchen. "The usual. Lots." She leaned against a cupboard and crossed her arms over her chest, still processing what had happened. With Jesse and his family. With her and Creed.

"You okay?" Jesse set the teapot on the stove. He turned on the burner.

Kat slapped away her thoughts. "Yeah. Of course." She was not about to let her brother worry over her. He was the one who had been in an accident.

Jesse opened a cabinet and pulled out a half-full bag of marshmallows. "You and Creed have a good talk?"

His question caught her off guard. It probably shouldn't have. Jesse had a sixth sense. He could read body language better than any man she'd ever met. It was one of the reasons he was such an incredible horse trainer. He understood communication without words, but Kat didn't always appreciate it when he turned his spidey senses on her.

"I guess." She shrugged one shoulder but gave up her façade when Jesse pressed her with knowing eyes. She swallowed and gave him the confirmation he was looking for. "Yeah. It was probably long overdue."

Jesse dug in the open cabinet. He retrieved two mugs and set them on the counter. "I'm glad." As he pulled two hot chocolate packets from the cabinet, he added, "It's nice to see you two in the same room together."

Her chest tightened. Creed was Jesse's best friend. It had hurt him to know that she and Creed had a troublesome past. Though he'd never say that to her. Kat also knew, if it came down to it, Jesse would choose her over Creed. Same with the rest of her family. And it would devastate them all. Which is why she'd never told *anyone* about the kiss that started the fight between her and Sarah.

Kat kept that secret. To protect Creed. To protect her family. No matter how much she ached, she never intended to throw that bomb out into the world.

Instead, she'd run away.

Kat gave her brother a hint of a smile and hoped that was all the information he needed. She didn't want to dig into the emotional conversation she'd had with Creed. She was still processing it herself.

Joining Jesse at the stove, Kat picked up the packets. She ripped them open and filled the mugs with chocolate powder. "Now, can you tell me all about my new niece or nephew? When is Hazel due? Do you guys have names picked out?"

The teapot whistled, and Kat pulled it from the burner. Jesse's face brightened, and a much happier conversation started. It continued well past their last sips of hot chocolate.

CHAPTER NINE

The next afternoon, Creed showed up at the Westons' to help decorate the flatbed trailer for the wedding. On Saturday, the trailer would serve as a shuttle from the front pasture—serving as a temporary parking lot—to the carriage house, where the wedding would take place.

"I still think you should let me and Evan throw you a bachelor party," Creed said to Jesse as they walked out of the barn, each carrying a bale of straw. They headed toward the trailer which was parked on the lawn between the barn and the house. It was hooked up to the tractor and edged with straw bales, which would serve as seating. Side boards rose above the straw, making perfect backrests. Hazel, Frankie, Anne, and Kat were decorating the trailer with streamers. "I think that's my duty as your best friend. You know I'd be good at it."

Jesse laughed. "I have no doubt you'd throw me a humdinger of a bachelor party, but I think we used up all our partying days in our twenties."

Creed chuckled. Jesse was right. "I think I've got a few left in me."

Jesse smirked. "Nah, I'm good. I've got all I need right there." He stared ahead at Hazel. She was laughing at something Frankie had said. Her face glowed, just like Jesse's. "I'm saving my celebrating for the reception."

"Okay," Creed said with mock disappointment. "If you change your mind, let me know." He shot Jesse a grin but was genuinely happy for his friend. Jesse had found his person.

Would Creed ever be as lucky?

"Throw those up here," Frankie called from on top of the trailer. "That should be all we need."

Jesse and Creed followed orders and tossed the straw bales onto the trailer. Then they hopped aboard and placed the bales where Frankie pointed, completing the seating arrangement.

"This is turning out *so* cute," Hazel said excitedly, stepping back to get a better look at the trailer.

Hazel and Anne had hung white and gold streamers around the wheelbase, like curtains. Frankie was adjusting the straw bales, pushing them snugly against the boarded sides of the trailer. Kat knelt on one of the bales and wrapped the top sideboard with a roll of gold streamer. A pile of white and gold rolls sat near her feet.

"Need some help?" Creed asked.

Kat glanced at him over her shoulder. "Sure. Want to start wrapping the bottom board in white?"

Creed grabbed a white roll and jumped off the trailer. He walked over to where Kat was working and started wrapping the lower board. Standing on the ground, he was face to face with Kat. Even when he wasn't looking at her, he could feel her gaze. Did she know the effect she had on him? He'd been pulled to her for what seemed like forever. At one time, Creed thought she'd be his person, that they'd end up together. Now that idea was just a fantasy.

Last night had been tough. He was grateful that they'd finally talked about the night Sarah passed, but he also knew words couldn't fix what happened. And the way Kat had cried nearly shattered him. When she had finally fallen asleep, he'd wanted to hold her all night. Instead, he laid her down on the couch, covered her with a blanket, and forced himself to move to the recliner. Kat was engaged, and Creed was not about to ruin her life, again. Holding her while she cried was one thing. Sleeping next to her was another.

He wrapped the white crepe paper around the board, searching for small talk to distract his mixed-up brain. "What'd you do this morning?"

"Took Thelma and Louise for a walk. Then I worked," Kat replied. Her hazel eyes were locked on the task at hand, but when her phone dinged, she retrieved it from the bale. "Speaking of." She gave a sigh and studied whatever was on her phone. It dinged two more times while she was staring at it. "My boss is relentless."

"Tell her to shove it," Creed said casually, and Kat surprised him with a laugh. It made him smile.

"I don't think she'd like that very much." Kat's smile disappeared as she typed a response on her phone. She set the phone back on the straw bale. "Looks like I'll be doing some more work tonight."

"Don't you have vacation days?"

"Technically, yes. I'm on vacation."

Creed was confused and annoyed that Kat's boss was bothering her when she was spending time with her family. "Why are you working, then? Seriously, tell her to shove it."

Kat smirked. "Maybe I will."

The Kat Creed had known would never hesitate to stand up for herself or for anyone she cared about. He'd seen her cuss Rick out quite a few times over the years. She wasn't a quiet bystander. If someone was out of line, she'd tell them so. Surely, Kat wouldn't let some corporate bully boss her around.

"I didn't think you took crap from anyone," he said. She'd never taken it from him.

Kat's face went serious. "I can't just tell her off."

"Why not?"

"First of all, I'd like to keep my job." She rolled the crepe paper around the board faster. "Second, I'm trying to get a promotion and I need my boss's recommendation to have a shot at it."

Creed nodded, but his stomach clenched as he realized Kat would hightail it out of Maple Bay right after Jesse's wedding. She had a life to go back to. He decided to change the subject.

"Have you done anything fun while you've been home?" he asked.

"Define fun."

"You played kickball. I witnessed that debauchery," he said.

Kat smiled at his use of the word *debauchery*. "That was fun." She slid him a sly grin. She was relishing her win.

"How about a four-wheeler ride? Gone out on the lake? Gone to get pizza at *Jake's*? Have you even stopped at *Patty Cakes* to get a maple bar?" At his last question, Kat's eyes shot to his like he'd just waved a donut in front of her face. "You seriously haven't gone to get a maple bar yet? You used to eat those like your life depended on it."

"I've been busy since I got here," Kat replied, sounding intrigued and annoyed all at once.

Hazel crept up next to Creed. She put a hand on his arm. "Did you guys say you're going to go get maple bars?" Hazel's eyes widened with hope.

"No, Creed was just giving me a hard time about—" Kat started, but Hazel's downturned lips cut her off.

"I could *really* use a maple bar. Or two. Would you guys mind going to get some?" Hazel whisper-asked, a plea in her tone. "And ask Patty to put a strip of bacon on one of the maple bars? I've got a serious craving for something sweet and salty."

Creed looked from Hazel to Kat. There was no way he was denying food to a pregnant lady.

"Sure." He sat the roll of crepe paper down on the trailer. "We can do that. Get a baker's dozen?"

Hazel nodded, enthusiastically.

"You don't need us to finish wrapping these boards?" Kat asked like her crepe-wrapping skills were highly sought after.

"Frankie, Anne, and I can finish. Besides, I think we all deserve a treat. And maple bars will definitely do the trick." Hazel spoke louder this time.

"Did you say maple bars?" Frankie called from over Kat's shoulder. "Oh boy. That sounds delish."

Kat set down the gold roll. She was now committed to getting donuts. "Okay, let's go." She gave Hazel a grin. "Maple bars for everyone!"

Hazel, Frankie, and Anne cheered. Kat laughed and stepped down from the trailer, joining Creed.

"We can take my truck if you don't mind walking to the lake," he said. It was a five-minute walk to the dock where he kept his houseboat and his truck.

Kat turned toward the barn. "We can take my rental car. I should probably do a test drive on that thing before I take it back to the airport Sunday night. Hopefully, it stays in one piece for the trip."

The ATV was parked at the front of the barn. "Want to take that? Like the old days?" He cocked his head, awaiting her answer. They used to drive the ATV into town all the time. Sometimes they rode horses. Both were completely acceptable to ride down Main Street in Maple Bay. "You remember how to have fun, don't you?" He was prodding her. She scrunched her face, and he knew it was working.

"I know how to have fun." Kat eyed the ATV as they neared it. It was a two-seater with a rollbar top and a tiny truck bed.

Creed slid in behind the steering wheel and cranked the key to start it. It purred to life. "Come on."

Kat crossed her arms. He thought she was going to shoot him down.

"If you think I'm going to let you drive, you're crazy. Scoot over." She shooed him with a hand.

Creed grinned and climbed over into the passenger seat. Mission accomplished. "It's all yours."

Kat hopped in. She put the ATV into gear, pressed the gas, and Creed suddenly remembered how she drove—like a bull bursting from a chute.

Creed's back slammed against the seat. "Whoa!" He grabbed the rollbar and gave Kat a sideways look that asked her if she was crazy. Then he laughed.

"Get ready for some *fun*," she taunted. They zipped down the gravel drive. "Keep your arms and legs in the vehicle at all times."

Kat took a sharp right off the drive, aiming for the shortcut between the two front pastures that led to the road. The force of her quick swerve pushed Creed smack against her. When their legs and shoulders clunked together, Creed automatically grabbed Kat's thigh, steadying them both. Her foot came off the gas, and they jerked to a stop on the front lawn. She looked at him, surprised, and Creed quickly realized it was from his touch. Probably not appropriate, but he held on. He considered holding on to her thigh for the rest of the ride in case he needed to manually redirect her foot to the brake. Plus . . . other reasons.

"Has your driving gotten worse since you moved to Chicago?" he asked.

Kat raised her brows. "I don't drive in Chicago."

"Ever?"

"I don't have a car. It's easy to get around without one." She looked down at his hand. It was still wrapped around her leg, just above her knee.

Creed let go and immediately smoothed over the awkward beat with sarcasm. "Are you sure you swerved to miss a deer on the way here? It wasn't just your rusty driving skills that put you in the field?"

Kat narrowed her eyes at him, though he caught a playful twinkle. "Scoot over and put your seatbelt on."

Creed did as he was told. "Do we need helmets?"

Kat put her seatbelt on as well and pressed the gas. "Only if you intend to keep up your sass-mouth."

Creed grinned. He'd missed Kat's quick wit. She'd always been able to match his banter.

They zoomed across the grass, in between the pastures, and rolled out onto the road that led to town. Cool fall air whipped around them like a tornado, and Creed glanced at Kat's smile a few times. It grew as they passed farmhouse after farmhouse. It was obvious to him that she'd needed a distraction from whatever was going on at work. When she parked on Main Street, next to the row of brick shops and striped awnings, Kat seemed looser, like she'd dropped her stresses somewhere on the way to town.

Creed unclipped his seatbelt. "We survived." He gave her a wink. She laughed, and they walked toward *Patty Cakes*.

The bakery was a corner shop, mostly comprised of a kitchen from which wafted the sweetest smells you could ever imagine. The storefront housed glass cases full of donuts and sugary treats. When Kat and Creed walked in, the three ladies behind the counter erupted into squeals. All three were good friends of Joyce. They gave Kat hugs and fawned over her like she was ten years old. She took it like a champ, answering the million questions they had for her. Creed grinned and leaned against the counter, watching the inquisition. When the questions ceased, Kat ordered a baker's dozen of maple bars.

"Patty, can you do a few of the bars with bacon?" Kat asked, standing at the cash register.

"You betcha," Patty replied. Rhonda and Beth were already filling up a box.

Kat turned to Creed. "Apple fritter for you?" she asked like they were out on a Sunday cruise and this was their usual stop. Like her mind had slipped over the five-year gap in which they hadn't spoken to or seen each other.

Creed cleared his throat. "Yes, please." Apple fritters were his favorite. He handed cash to Patty.

"You don't need to do that." Kat tipped her head at him.

"Consider it bribery so you don't crash us on the way home."

Kat cracked a grin. "Bribe taken." She took the box of donuts from Patty, said her goodbyes, and Creed followed her outside, onto the sidewalk.

"Want to eat our donuts before we go back?" he asked. "You know I can't ignore that fritter for long." The sweet smell of fresh baked goods was too great a temptation.

"Sure. I could use some sugar." Kat glanced around. The inside of *Patty Cakes* didn't have seating. There were two bistro tables outside on the sidewalk, but both were filled. Kat shrugged. "Go down by the lake?"

Creed agreed, and they crossed the road to amble down a small, sandy slope toward the lake. Kat took a seat on a big rock, set the donut box on her lap, and opened it. Creed sat down next to her on a wide tree stump. She handed him his apple fritter and a napkin, and they bit into their chosen pastries.

Kat's eyes fluttered as she chewed. "This is like heaven." She licked her lips, and Creed diverted his eyes before they locked into a stare. He took a big bite of his fritter and glanced out over the lake.

"I almost forgot how beautiful it is here in the fall," Kat said.

"It sure is." Red, yellow, and orange leaves topped all the trees edging the dark waters of Maple Leaf Lake. A flock of geese squawked and circled in the sky. A fishing boat purred in the distance. Maple Bay was like chicken soup for the soul, no matter the season.

"Chicago's beautiful too, but in a different way," she added.

Creed rested an elbow on his knee. "How so?" He'd never cared for the crammed spaces and constant noise of big cities.

Kat straightened her legs out in front of her and crossed them at her ankles, as though she hadn't stretched in a while. "I guess the beauty is in the experience. The endless amounts of restaurants. The theater. Museums. There's a lot to do."

A squirrel ran by and chirped a warning at them. Was the little gray creature reminding Creed that Kat had a fiancé? That he was probably a sophisticated museum-goer and the exact opposite of Creed?

"Is Michael from Chicago?" he asked.

Kat took a big bite of her donut instead of answering. He squinted at her even though she wasn't looking at him. It seemed like Kat had been avoiding questions about her fiancé this week. And it wasn't just the questions he asked. He'd watched her dance around questions from her mom, aunts, and sister. Was she uncomfortable talking about Michael with Creed around? He didn't want her to clam up on his account.

"Yes, he's from Chicago," she spoke through a mouthful of donut. "He grew up just outside the city, in Naperville. His parents still live there. And he has two sisters that live in the city too."

The first major piece of information she'd given up.

"Will you guys live in Chicago after you get married?"

Kat brought her legs back in, close to the rock. "Probably. We both have established jobs there. I can't see us moving somewhere else." Then, for whatever reason, she redirected the conversation to Creed's relationship status. "What about your girlfriend? Where'd you meet her?"

Creed assumed she was referring to Zoey. He finished his last bite of fritter and wiped his fingers with a napkin. "You mean Zoey?"

Kat nodded. She tucked her hair behind her ears.

"We date, but she's not my girlfriend."

"No chance she'll settle you down?" Kat's question ran over him like rough sandpaper.

"Oh, you know me," he replied, brushing it off. "Not much of the settling down kind." He leaned forward, putting both forearms on his knees and making a point of looking at the fishing boat in the distance, instead of Kat.

His statement was only half true. He wasn't the settling down kind, but that was only because no one had ever grabbed him like Kat. The only woman that had ever made Creed want to settle down was sitting next to him, perched on a rock, eating a maple bar, getting ready to take another man's last name.

Kat twisted her lips. "Well, Zoey might be a little more involved than you are. Just FYI."

Creed squinted at her. "What do you mean?"

"She's got you tagged in, like, a million photos." Kat was looking at Creed like he might be the most oblivious man in the world. "On Facebook. Lots of pictures from rodeos. And the lake."

"Huh," Creed replied, gears turning in his head. He didn't know that, but he was rarely on Facebook. And wouldn't Kat have had to do a little digging around to notice that? "Facebook-stalking me, were you?"

"What? No." Kat's cheeks went rosy. "I was just curious who she was. Looking out for you. That's it. You need a good girl."

Creed nodded. It wasn't like he hadn't Facebook-stalked Kat before. Sometimes he peeked at her pictures when he was feeling low. Her bright smile always cheered him up. "I've got it handled. Don't you worry." He smiled at her.

Kat popped the last piece of maple bar into her mouth. "You ready? We better get back before Hazel's sugar-salt craving gets out of control."

They stood and walked back to the ATV in an awkward silence. After taking their seats, Creed strapped on his seatbelt and Kat handed him the box of donuts to hold.

The whole ride back, he couldn't help but wonder if he'd caught a hint of jealousy in Kat's questions and Facebook investigation. But if he had, what the heck did it mean?

CHAPTER TEN

After Kat and Creed delivered donuts to the trailer-decorating crew, Kat made an excuse to slink away to the house. Or, more properly, hide there. She said she had to answer work emails—which she did—but mostly she needed to get away from Creed's knowing eyes. She could've kicked herself when she mentioned the tagged photos on Facebook. She'd been trying to get Creed to quit asking questions about her nonexistent fiancé. Instead, she'd waved a huge red flag that said, *I'm the crazy ex that's secretly stalking you on social media.* Kat knew she shouldn't have been poking around last night, looking at Creed's Facebook on her phone. She was so careful to keep her scrolling finger on the far side of the screen, preventing any chance of an accidental "like." Then she just had to open her mouth today.

"Ugh," Kat grunted as she stepped into the kitchen. Thelma and Louise jumped from the couch and ran to greet her. She picked them up, putting each wiggly dog under an arm, and proceeded to kiss their whiskered noses. They licked her face, and Kat instantly felt relief.

"You two are the best." She kissed them each one more time before setting them down. "Cuddle time while Momma does emails?" Both dogs excitedly followed her upstairs where the three of them got situated on the bed. Kat powered up her computer and set it on her lap. Thelma and Louise curled into little balls on each side of her.

As her laptop started up, Kat pulled her phone from her sweatshirt pocket and jumped when she saw how many text messages she had. "What the?" She'd turned her phone on silent after Creed razzed her about her boss's antics.

Kat scrolled through at least ten texts, all from Lei. The texts got progressively more urgent. They started with a standard "SOS," moved to some dramatic emoji strings, and ended with a few aggressive GIFs. The last one said "CALL ME" in all caps.

Kat immediately video-called Lei on her laptop. The WiFi was better than the spotty cell phone coverage she got in her parents' house.

Lei picked up in one ring. Her face was close to the camera. "Where have you been?" Her eyes were wide, peering over her red rimmed glasses. She didn't look like she was in the office, even though it was only three o'clock on a Wednesday.

"What's wrong?" Kat asked. Lei could be dramatic, but an SOS text was serious business. They only sent those to each other when immediate action was needed. "Are you at the bar?" Kat recognized the red vinyl booth Lei was sitting in. She was at their favorite place—a Mexican restaurant just down the block from the office that had the best margaritas.

"I had to get out of the office. Told my boss I needed an extra-long lunch because I had cramps. Lady cramps. He practically seized up and told me to take as long of a lunch as I wanted, which was good because it's taken me a whole hour to get ahold of you." She raised a coffee cup in front of the laptop. "And I'm not drinking. Not yet anyhow." She raised an eyebrow.

"What happened?"

Lei set the cup back down. "Wendy has lost her ever-lovin' mind."

Kat groaned. "What'd she do now?"

"I was making copies and could hear her talking in her office. Her door was open. She mentioned *Midwest Farm & Home,* and I know that's the account you've been working forever to land, so I stayed at the copier and eavesdropped. Kat, she was talking with the buyer for *Midwest Farm & Home.* I couldn't hear much of the conversation, but I thought you should know right away. Why would she be talking to him?"

Kat's mouth dropped. She had no idea why Wendy would be on the phone with her account. Correction: *potential* account. Kat had an appointment with the buyer for *Midwest Farm & Home* next week. She'd been working on her presentation for months.

"I don't know," Kat said. Then her heart started to pound. She picked her phone back up and made a high-pitched squeak when she saw the voicemail notification.

Kat looked at Lei. "There's a voicemail from the buyer at *Midwest.*"

Lei leaned so close to the camera that Kat could only see her glasses. "Listen to it!"

Kat played the voicemail and put her phone on speaker. The words were choppy because of the spotty cell service, but the essence of the message was that her appointment for next week was cancelled. The buyer said that his company and *Genius Appliances* were not aligned, and he didn't think doing business together was a good choice for either company.

"No," Kat yelled. Her stomach flopped.

Lei's mouth was open. Her chin nearly rested on her keyboard. Kat was sure she looked the same.

"What the heck?" Lei exclaimed.

"What did she say to him?" Kat sputtered. "I've been trying to get an appointment with that buyer for a year now. Wendy knows that. Why would she go over my head?" What would Wendy even have to say to the buyer at this point?

"She's so shifty." Lei spoke like she was scolding a naughty puppy. "She's always got to toot her own horn. Maybe she was trying to steal your spotlight?"

Kat was confused. Was Wendy trying to take credit for landing the account? If so, what had she said to make the buyer cancel her upcoming meeting?

"Lei, I've got to call—" Kat started, but Lei's face disappeared. It was replaced by an extremely obnoxious message—that a restart was needed in order to install updates. Two seconds later, Kat's laptop shutdown. The screen went black. "Oh no!" Why did that always happen at the *worst* possible time? When the spinning wheel of death appeared on the screen, Kat knew her laptop would be out of order for a good half hour. She snatched her phone from the quilt, needing to call Wendy, to find out what was going on before she reached out to the client. It wouldn't look good if Kat called the client and was totally unaware of his conversation with her boss.

Kat dialed Wendy's office, but the cell reception was so weak that the call wouldn't go through. Kat grunted, wishing she'd connected her phone to her parent's WiFi. The passcode was some crazy mixture of numbers and letters, like her dad was trying to keep Russia from tapping into his internet connection. He was the only one that knew the passcode, and he wasn't home.

Needing to get to a location with better cell reception, Kat popped off the bed, ran downstairs, and scooted outside. Thelma and Louise followed her, thinking they were off on an adventure. In the backyard, Kat walked around aimlessly, trying to get a better signal on her phone. Her dogs ventured behind her, prancing through the grass.

"Dang it," she said, holding her phone above her head and peering at the screen.

"Trying to make a call?" Creed's voice boomed from a distance.

Kat pulled her eyes from her phone. Creed was sitting on the tractor next to the barn. It looked like he'd just parked the decorated hay trailer.

"Yeah. Where is everyone?" Kat continued walking, moving closer to Creed and the barn. Still, she couldn't get a decent signal.

"Went to pick up the kids from school."

Kat squinted at her phone, wondering if nasty looks would help. "Why is the cell service so bad here? I don't remember it ever being this bad."

"What service do you have?"

"Celleband." She'd switched phone carriers a year ago. She'd never had this problem in Chicago.

Creed made a face like that was bad news. "You'll probably get better service on the lake."

"*On* the lake?"

"There's a clear line of sight to a cell tower or something out toward the middle of the lake. I swear. I can take you out on my boat if you want. Or you can use my phone." He walked toward her. Thelma ran at him, barking playfully. Creed reached down and scratched her head.

"Would you mind taking me out on your boat?" she asked. "I have a really important call I have to make for work." Kat didn't figure Wendy would answer a number she didn't recognize.

Creed shrugged. "No problem. Let's go."

They walked past the barn, toward the lake. Thelma ran a few fast laps around them. Louise was being pokey, sniffing every blade of grass, so Kat picked her up. Louise really didn't like to walk anyhow. She was much happier in Kat's arms.

"You look really serious." Creed said when they got to the dock. He picked up Thelma and carried her onto the boat.

Kat followed with Louise. "Kind of have a major issue at work. Need to figure it out before it gets any worse." Her mind was coming unhinged. Had a year's worth of work come undone because her boss said something she shouldn't have?

Creed entered his houseboat. Kat stepped in behind him, into his kitchen. He handed Thelma to her.

"I'll be right back. Just need to untie the boat and we can get going." Creed stepped out and onto the dock, where he unhooked the ropes that kept the boat in place. Then he took his place behind the steering wheel on the front deck, pressed a few buttons, and started the motor. Soon they were leaving the dock and humming along the water like a pontoon. If Kat hadn't been so worried about work stuff, she would've enjoyed the ride. Instead, she set her dogs down and took a seat on Creed's couch to stare at her phone. Thelma and Louise happily explored their new digs.

As the boat started to slow, Kat watched her cell phone signal go to five bars.

"Got it!" she called to Creed. She popped up from the couch and paced back and forth as she called her boss. Every ring tightened her anxiety. When her call went to voicemail, Kat nearly screamed. Wendy's message said she'd be out of the office the rest of the day with no access to phone or email.

"No!" Kat whacked her hand to her forehead just as Creed opened the door.

"What now?" he asked, still standing in the doorway.

"I can't get ahold of my boss."

Creed looked lost. "Is it something that can't wait until Monday? I thought you were on vacation until—"

"No, Creed! It can't wait!" All the anxiety she'd been trying to control fizzled into her response. She instantly felt bad for shouting at Creed but had no time to say so because an orange ball of fur came trotting out of Creed's bedroom.

Kat had almost forgotten about Creed's cat, but when Sasquatch meowed to make his presence known, Thelma turned into a Tasmanian Devil. Her little terrier feet bounced forward with such force that she ran in place for a few strides before racing at Sasquatch. The cat arched his back and hissed but didn't wait to see if the little spotted dog was a valid threat. Instead, Sasquatch jumped onto the kitchen counter and blazed a trail. He leapt over the sink, knocked down a box of cereal, and flew across the room to land on the table, like Spiderman.

"Thelma!" Kat scolded as her dog relentlessly barked and chased the cat. She tried to catch Thelma but her dog was bouncing around like a rubber ball. Thelma was on a mission and didn't seem to notice that Kat was yelling at her. Louise joined in on the barking, egging on her sister.

"Whoa!" Creed called and lurched forward in a dazed attempt to stop the craziness. Kat wasn't sure if he was trying to catch Sasquatch or Thelma, but both animals shot around him like pinballs and sailed out the open door.

Kat screamed as the chase continued onto the small deck. She and Creed scrambled outside just in time to watch Sasquatch jump onto the deck railing. He landed on top of the metal rail and ran across it nimbly, like a gymnast. Thelma scrambled to join him. She launched herself onto a bench and jumped for the railing. She aimed her jump at Sasquatch but did *not* hit her target. Instead, Thelma went flying over the railing and into the lake.

Kat vaguely heard Creed yell, though she didn't comprehend a word he said. Kat had only just adopted Thelma a few months ago. She had never had her around water and had no idea if her little dog could swim.

Panicked, Kat took two big steps, vaulted herself over the railing, and plunged into the dark, cold lake. When she was fully submerged, Kat opened her eyes. Underwater, she couldn't see more than ten feet. She spun to the right and then to the left, searching for Thelma. What if she couldn't find her? What if she couldn't save her?

Fear engulfed her like the lake, and she nearly lost her breath when she glimpsed a white-and-brown-spotted body paddling like the dickens. *Thelma.* Kat swam forward with a few quick strokes, reaching Thelma just as her dog broke the surface of the lake. Kat emerged as well, with a big gasp, ready to grab hold of her dog. But Thelma was just fine. She barked and doggy-paddled toward Kat, surprised to see her mom burst out of the lake. Then, like they were playing the best game ever, Thelma barked and swam a circle around Kat, much like she did on the ground.

"You little minx," Kat said with a sigh. Treading water, she spun back toward the boat and discovered that Creed had jumped into the lake too. He was treading water as well, not far from where she was. They locked eyes, peering over the lake at each other. Thelma swam between them, completing her circle. She barked again. Louise returned Thelma's bark from the boat.

At that, Creed cracked a smile. Kat's relief surfaced in a laugh. Then she got lake water in her mouth and coughed.

"Come on." Creed chuckled. "Let's get you both back on the boat."

"I can't believe that just happened." Kat swam toward Creed and the boat, watching to make sure Thelma followed her.

"I wish I had that on video so we could replay it in slow motion." Creed got to the boat first and grabbed hold of the metal ladder that led to the deck. "You go up first. I'll hand you Thelma."

Kat took hold of the ladder and pulled herself up, rung by rung. On the boat, her drenched sweatshirt and jeans poured a puddle onto the deck. She turned back to Creed. He was hanging onto the ladder with one hand and holding Thelma out with the other. He palmed her ribcage, and Thelma continued to doggy-paddle, convinced she might go back in the water. Her brown eyes were wild with excitement.

"Oh, you naughty little dog." Kat took hold of Thelma and pressed her to her chest. She peppered her with kisses and thanked the Lord that her dog could swim.

Creed climbed out of the lake and joined Kat on the deck. They took one look at each other and started belly laughing.

"You didn't tell me your dog was a cat killer," Creed jested, yanking off a leather boot. Water sloshed out of it, along with a piece of seaweed.

"I didn't know." Kat wrung out her hair, still holding Thelma in case Sasquatch was in sight. "I just adopted her a few months ago. I've never had her around a cat. I wasn't sure she could swim either. I about had a heart attack when she went into the lake."

"Hey, Thelma." Creed peered at the rascally dog in Kat's arms. "Sasquatch is actually a pretty nice cat if you just get to know him." Thelma's pink tongue hung out. She was panting but seemed thoroughly proud of herself for chasing off the orange monster.

Kat shook her head at her dog. "You just caused quite the ruckus." She glanced around. "I'm not sure I should let her down. I think she'll just chase Sasquatch again."

Creed ran a hand through his blond hair, which was now dark and dripping wet. "Nah, she's fine. Sasquatch is up on the rooftop deck now." He pointed up and Kat saw a glimpse of an orange tail through a wooden railing. She covered Thelma's eyes so her rascally dog didn't see the tail as well. Creed smirked. "I'll close the hatch inside. He can stay up there for now."

"I feel bad locking your cat out of his house because Thelma has no manners." She gave Creed an apologetic look.

"Don't feel bad. He loves it on the roof, especially when the sun's out. He's a professional sunbather. Plus, he's not dripping wet like we are."

She gave Creed a smile. "Thanks for jumping in." He had his cowboy boots off, but his hooded sweatshirt and jeans clung to him. He stood, socks soaking wet, in a growing puddle. "And I'm sorry I yelled at you. I shouldn't have taken my work frustrations out on you." Kat had snapped at Creed for something that was totally not his fault. Then he'd turned around and dove into the lake to save her dog.

What a man he was.

"Not a big deal." He wrung out the front of his sweatshirt. "But Thelma might owe me a box of Captain Crunch." He winked, and Kat looked through the window, remembering the cereal box that had toppled over in the cat-dog chase. Round cereal was scattered all over the floor. A lamp and a few couch pillows were also casualties.

Kat shook her head at Thelma again. "I'll clean that up."

"How about we change into dry clothes first?"

Caution signs glowed in Kat's head. "Oh, no. That's okay. I'm fine." Which was an absolutely silly response. She'd jumped into a Minnesota lake in October. Her fully drenched, cold clothes were pulling her body temperature down by the second.

Creed cocked his head at her. "I've got clothes you can wear. Honestly, you don't need to hang out in wet jeans."

Hang out? Was that what they were doing?

Creed stepped inside, not waiting for her to answer. "I'm not going to be responsible for you catching a cold and being sick for your brother's wedding."

Kat cautiously followed him into the cabin and closed the door behind her, locking both Thelma and Louise inside. Creed disappeared into the backside of the boat and reappeared with a couple of towels.

"One for you and one for Thelma." He handed a towel to Kat. Then he took Thelma from her, wrapping the little dog in a fuzzy towel. "I'll dry her off while you get changed. I put some clothes on my bed."

Creed patted Thelma dry with the towel. Kat's heart ignored all the caution signs in her head and literally melted. She could've watched the cuteness for days. Instead, she scooted by Creed before he saw her thoughts on her face. "Thank you."

Walking to the back of the boat, Kat stepped into Creed's bedroom. She pulled the curtain closed between the bedroom and the rest of the boat. His room was mostly filled by a big bed made up in dark-navy sheets and a matching comforter. The back wall held shelves filled with books, belt buckles, and mementos. There was a metal spiral staircase in the corner that led to a door in the ceiling. It must've been the hatch that led to the rooftop deck. When Kat's eyes fell again to the messed bedding, she pictured Creed wrapped in the sheets, kicking his leg out of the bedding because he was always too hot. She knew he slept only in briefs . . . Kat took a quick breath. What was she doing?

She rubbed her temples and told herself to change into the dry stack of clothes Creed had left on his bed. *Fast.* She was simply on a boat with an old friend. Nothing else. Except this old friend was also an ex-boyfriend. Someone she'd once been madly in love with. And she was about to strip down and put on his clothes.

"Will those work?" Creed called, and Kat jumped.

"Yep," she replied before digging into the clothes. Quickly, Kat yanked her wet, heavy sweatshirt over her head. She peeled off her jeans and unstuck her sports bra and granny panties, making a mental note to go underwear shopping next week. She needed at least a *few* pairs of underwear that were somewhat cute.

After patting herself dry with the towel, Kat pulled on the sweatshirt Creed had set out. It was huge. Kat could've worn it as a dress, but she wasn't about to do that. Determined to cover herself up, she pulled on the sweatpants as well. Then she cinched the waist tight and rolled up the pant legs. She felt like a kid playing dress-up, but it was nice to get out of her wet clothes.

Kat gathered her pile of dripping clothes from the floor, making sure to hide her granny panties. "Where should I put these? I don't want them dripping all over your house." She pushed the curtain aside and stepped out of the bedroom. She almost fell over when she saw Creed. He was kneeling next to the couch, shirtless, tending to Thelma and Louise. Both her dogs were wrapped in towels. Creed had them bundled up next to each other on the couch, like little burritos. *Pup-urritos.*

"I'll hang them on the deck," Creed offered, and scratched both dogs on their heads. When he glanced Kat's way, he shrugged his toned shoulders. "Louise seemed jealous, so I got her a towel too."

Kat had no words. The insane amount of sexy and cute had closed her throat and sent her brain into a spin.

Creed stood, and Kat wondered if he'd gotten even better looking with age. How had he managed that? It was like the extra years had perfected every muscle. His strapping chest. Chiseled abs. The way his wet jeans hung low on his hips . . . Kat suddenly realized her eyes had taken their very own road trip down Creed's middle. She popped her gaze back up to Creed's face and found him staring at her, wearing a smug grin.

"I'll take those." He reached for her wet clothes. She jerked back.

"I got it." She scooted past him, much like Sasquatch and Thelma had earlier, nearly bouncing off his chest on the way by. "You go get dressed." She absolutely did not need that mouthwatering, smug distraction within reach. "Put on a shirt," she awkwardly added as she flew through the door and onto the deck.

Get ahold of yourself, Kat told her traitorous body. *Falling back into those arms is a bad idea. A really bad idea.*

Kat hung her soaked clothes over the railing and stuffed her unmentionables into her wet sweatshirt pocket. As she did, she eyed Creed's cowboy boots and reminded herself that those boots were made for walking. He didn't stay in one place for long. He didn't set down roots. Not with a woman. And especially not with her. She was not about to let him pull her in, capture her heart, and break it into a million pieces. She'd be a fool if she let that happen for a third time.

Considering her muddled brain, Kat thought about diving into the cold lake one more time . . . just to clear her head.

CHAPTER ELEVEN

Creed knew he was treading in deep water. And it had nothing to do with his impromptu dip in the lake and everything to do with the woman sitting on his couch, staring at her phone, pretending like she hadn't just looked him up and down with fire in her eyes. Her wandering glance had kickstarted his heart, but Creed quickly squashed any idea of moving past a heated glance. Kat was engaged. He wanted to see her happy, and if she'd chosen another man, he needed to accept that. She'd chosen someone more suitable for her. Creed's chance was gone. He could be her friend, and even that would be a miracle after what they'd been through together.

"You know it is five o'clock, right?" Creed asked, now in a dry flannel shirt and jeans. "I think you can stop working."

Kat gave him a sideways glance and kept tapping away at her phone. "I just have to finish this email and then I'll be done." She tapped some more. Then her phone made a swooshing sound. "There. All done. Not anything else I can do until tomorrow." She sighed and set her phone on the couch, next to Thelma and Louise, who were now sleeping. They were still wrapped in their towels.

"Join me on the roof for happy hour?" Creed opened his fridge and pulled out a jug with a recognizable label. He knew it'd get Kat's attention. "I have root beer." Her eyebrows rose. The jug was half full of homemade root beer from *Lakeside*—a drive-in diner on the north side of the lake. Their homemade root beer was a local delicacy.

When Kat didn't immediately agree, Creed went for her Achilles' heel. "And I think you should make up with Sasquatch. He's probably feeling like a total outcast by himself on the roof."

She peered at him. Her lips turned down at the edges. "You said he liked it up there."

He did. Sasquatch was perfectly happy on the roof. "I'm sure he'd appreciate a little company. Especially after being assaulted by your killer dog." Creed took two glasses out of a cabinet and started filling one with root beer. By the time he topped off the glass, Kat had risen from the couch.

"Okay. One drink." She joined him at the counter.

"One drink." Creed handed her the full glass.

Kat took a sip, and her amber eyes sparkled. "Reminds me of summer," she said, and her throat made a purring noise.

Creed's pulse quickened, and he turned away to fill the other glass. "Me too," he agreed. More so, it reminded him of her. Kat and Creed had sipped *Lakeside* root beer just about every day the summer after Kat's senior year. The summer Creed had been able to call Kat his girlfriend.

That summer had been both wonderful and awful. Creed and Kat had started dating in secret, because Creed hadn't wanted to admit to Jesse or Evan that he was in love with their little sister. He'd been in love with Kat for years but had always steered clear of pursuing her for fear of causing a rift with the Weston family. Gene and Joyce were the closest thing he had to parents. Jesse and Evan were his best friends. He considered them brothers. Creed knew he wasn't exactly ideal boyfriend material, so he wasn't surprised when the Westons freaked out when Kat told them she was dating him. Evan took a swing at Creed. Jesse didn't talk to Creed for weeks. Gene and Joyce sat Creed down and let him know he was not to mess with their daughter's heart. Creed understood their worries, but it still hurt.

But regardless of what her family said, Kat stood by Creed. She never wavered in what she wanted—to be with him—and her family came around to the idea of them together. Though that only made his decision harder at the end of the summer. Creed knew he had to break up with her. He didn't have a choice. Kat was smart, witty, outgoing. She had a full-ride scholarship to the University of

Wisconsin and a lifetime of opportunities ahead of her. But if he'd let her, she would have thrown that all away to stay with him. For what? To follow him to rodeos? To live with him in a horse trailer? She deserved more than he could give her. If he hadn't broken her heart—and his own—she wouldn't have gone off to college.

Instead of saying that, Creed clinked her glass with his. "Cheers."

"Cheers," Kat replied, and they both took a drink.

"Now, let's go visit Sasquatch." Creed turned, stepped into his bedroom, and started up the stairs. After pushing open the hatch door, he crawled onto the roof deck. Then he took Kat's hand to help her up as well. He let go as soon as she had both feet on the roof, not wanting to linger.

Sasquatch greeted them. He was sprawled across the padded lounge chair where Creed spent most evenings winding down. The cat jumped down from the chair and pranced over. He gave them a few meows.

"Hey, bud." Creed petted him from his head to his tail. He started to purr. "This is the momma of the rascally visitors." Creed gave Kat a grin, letting her know he was just giving her a hard time.

"Hi, Sasquatch." Kat offered the cat her hand, and Sasquatch rubbed his whiskered face against it, soaking up the attention. "I'm so sorry about Thelma. We didn't mean to scare you."

He meowed again, and Kat continued to make peace by scratching and petting Sasquatch until his purring was so loud that it rivaled a motorboat.

"I think he forgives you," Creed said and sat in one of the chairs next to a round table.

Kat joined him, sitting cross-legged on the other chair. "I sure hope so." Sasquatch jumped into her lap and curled up. "Oh good. Now I have a lap warmer." She smiled.

"Are you cold? You want a jacket?" It was maybe fifty degrees, but the temperature was bound to drop quickly. The sun was setting, casting a warm glow over the still lake. Creed got up.

"No, I'm fine. I promise. Your sweats are plenty warm." She took a drink of root beer and set the glass on the table. Her fingers barely poked out of the sleeves, and Creed liked the way his clothes draped her like a blanket. She used to steal his jean jacket at rodeos. It had looked better on her than it ever did on him.

"Do you remember the rowboat?" Kat asked, surprising him with a memory from high school.

"The one Evan flipped when he tried to fit half the football team on it?"

Kat laughed. She pulled her still-wet hair over her shoulder. "Yeah, that one. That boat was not meant to carry six large linebackers." Kat smiled, remembering. "But it sure gave us all a lot of fun times on the sandbar."

"It did," Creed agreed, remembering the sandbar—one of the islands in the middle of the lake—where he'd spent many summer days with the Weston kids and various friends. They'd swim, play football, soak up the sun, and spend the evening around a campfire. The sandbar had also been where Kat had taken Creed many times when he'd needed a break from his dad. They'd sit under the stars. Sometimes with a campfire. Sometimes simply sharing silence. She'd been his rock a lot more than she knew.

"This was a great place to grow up," Kat said as the sun inched lower, dipping the colorful autumn leaves in peach. Then pink. Then gold.

"It's a pretty great place to live now." Creed ran a finger over the rim of his glass. He bounced from rodeo to rodeo, living between his boat and truck, but Maple Bay would always be the place he considered home. It was the place that held the people he cared most about. It wasn't a house, building, or a job that always called him back. It was the people.

Kat didn't respond. At least not with words.

Creed's breathing slowed. He wanted to ask Kat if she would've stayed in Maple Bay if Sarah hadn't tragically passed. Would she have stayed with *him* if that one night hadn't happened? But he didn't. Creed couldn't toss those painful memories back at Kat. He didn't want to see pain on her face, especially when she looked so serene in the golden glow of the sunset.

Kat finished the last gulp of her root beer and set the empty glass on the table. "We should get going. I told Mom I'd help her make pies for the groom's supper. She was going to start after dinner."

Creed wanted to keep Kat captive on his boat, but knew it wasn't in the cards. "Yeah, we should get going. It's getting dark, and Sasquatch won't want to stay up here if he can't sunbathe."

Kat stood. She set Sasquatch down on the chair and gave him a pet. "Thanks for sharing your boat with my pups. We'll get back to the dock so you can get comfortable in your nice, warm home. Okay?"

Sasquatch rubbed his head against her hand and meowed.

Creed gathered both glasses and walked over to the hatch door. He went down first, so he could turn on a light. His bedroom was dark, and the spiral stairs were a little tricky to navigate if you weren't used to them. But he wasn't quite fast enough. Kat started down the stairs, and Creed clicked on the bedside lamp just in time to see her stumble. The sweatpants she'd borrowed had unrolled, and Kat's foot caught in the loose leg. Suddenly, she toppled down the stairs like she'd stepped in a hole.

Creed dropped the glasses. They hit the carpet as he lurched toward Kat. Miraculously, he caught her. Stupidly, he wasn't prepared for what she'd feel like in his arms.

Kat fell against him with a hard umph, much like she had on the kickball field. But this time, Creed wrapped his arms around her and pressed her flush against his chest. Her hands fumbled before finding themselves on his shoulders. Her feet were still on the stairs. If he hadn't been there, she would've fallen flat on the floor.

When she picked her head up and looked him in the eye, Creed's heart flipped. He wanted to kiss her. He wanted to spin her around and pin her to his bed, find out if she still tasted the same. Everything inside him screamed. There was an entire herd of wild mustangs captured in his chest, eager to escape.

Kat's lips parted, and for a second, he thought she wanted to kiss him too.

"Creed, I—" she started.

Creed caught the flash of guilt in her amber eyes, and he pushed down every urge he'd just felt. *This is not okay.* No matter how he felt. Kat had a ring on her finger. She was ready to start her life with someone else.

"Those stairs are tricky." Creed's voice was raspy. He wondered if Kat caught the disappointment behind his words. He helped her stand upright. When her feet were on the ground, he said, "You good?"

Kat nodded. Creed let her go. Then he gave her a tight smile and got out of the bedroom quickly. He needed to get back to the dock.

CHAPTER TWELVE

Kat opened the front door to her parents' house and slipped inside, feeling like she was sixteen again and sneaking in past curfew. She held a bundle of wet clothes, both her dogs were at her heels, and she wanted to get upstairs without being seen. The kitchen was full of chatting, pie-making Weston ladies, and Kat could only imagine the inquisition she'd endure if she was caught wearing Creed's clothes. Her mom, sister, and aunts would corner her and make her squeal, but she wasn't sure *what* she'd squeal to them. The boat ride had scrambled her brain, like a shot of tequila. She was warm and fuzzy, but also wary of the headache she'd have in the morning.

Avoiding an inquisition, Kat tiptoed through the entryway like a burglar and quickened her pace when she hit the stairs. She shot up the staircase, skipping steps she knew were squeaky. When she hit the last stair, Kat took a breath, thinking she was safe. Then she rounded the corner into the hall and ran straight into a roadblock.

She collided with her cousin, Myra.

"Whoa!" Myra said as she bounced off Kat. Kat toppled and caught herself on a wall. Myra stumbled back into the bathroom she'd just come out of. "Geez, what you running from?"

"Nothing," Kat said, knowing she'd just been caught red-handed.

Myra got her footing and ran her eyes up and down Kat. A few times. She cocked her head. Then an eyebrow. "*Where'd* you come from?" Her question was way too loud.

"*Nowhere*," Kat replied, but Myra knew her better than that.

"What do you mean *nowhere*?"

Myra's mom, Judy, called up the stairs, "You okay up there? What'd you do? Fall off the toilet?"

Myra rolled her eyes and jerked a thumb toward the staircase. "She acts like I'm still four. Or worse, eighty." She called back to her mom. "Didn't fall off the toilet, Mom. I'll be down in a second."

"Well, quit dillydallying. We got pies to make," Judy replied, her voice dwindling as she retreated from the stairwell.

Kat let out a breath and pushed herself off the wall. She picked up her wet jeans which had fallen to the floor.

"So, are you going to tell me what you were up to?" Myra gave her a curious smile.

"It's a long story." Kat scooted down the hall, avoiding Myra's prodding. She wanted to get changed before the whole crew of Weston ladies charged upstairs.

Myra followed Kat into the bedroom. "I love long stories." She closed the door and spun toward Kat. "Why are you wearing Creed's clothes?"

"What?" Kat squeaked, stunned by her cousin's sleuthing skills.

Myra quirked her lips. "Kat, the back of the sweatshirt you're wearing has Creed's name on it."

How had she missed that? Kat slapped her forehead and dropped the wad of wet clothes she'd been carrying. When they hit the carpet, her clothes rolled open, and Kat's wrinkled, wet granny panties toppled out. Myra's mouth popped open, and Kat knew she had to tell her cousin the truth, else she'd come to her own conclusions.

"It's not what you think." Kat turned to the twin bed behind her, which held her open suitcase. She dug through her suitcase and grabbed the first shirt, yoga pants, and underwear she came across. "I was on Creed's boat. Thelma chased his cat and then fell into the lake. We both jumped in to save her. Except she's a good swimmer and really didn't need to get saved. She was fine, but we were both soaked. Creed gave me dry clothes to wear, except his legs are like double the length of mine and I tripped over a pant leg and fell into his arms and almost kissed him." Kat froze, feeling like she'd just vomited all over. She had. Verbal vomit.

Thelma stretched lazily on the bed like she hadn't been the instigator of the fiasco. Then she curled up next to Louise, who was already burrowed into the quilt.

"Uh, wow. That was a lot of information," Myra replied. She walked over and sat on the other bed. "I have questions . . . but did you say that you *almost* kissed Creed?"

Kat had mixed feelings about what she'd just rehashed. "Yes. *Almost.*"

She had also *almost* told Creed that she wasn't engaged, that she and Michael had parted ways. She'd *almost* told him that she was wearing her engagement ring like a life vest, not wanting to drown in a sea of unknowns and what-ifs. When she'd landed in Creed's arms, emotions had stirred and she had *almost* told him how much she'd missed him, how mad she'd been that her whole world had exploded, that she had to rebuild it without him. But as soon as she opened her mouth, Creed had pulled back. He'd set her on the ground and walked away.

Kat looked from her messy suitcase to Myra. Her cousin was sitting on the bed, her back against the headboard. When they made eye contact, Myra leaned forward.

"Are you okay?" Myra asked. She didn't ask why Kat had almost kissed her ex. She didn't remind Kat that she had a fiancé.

Kat huffed and sat down on the bed, next to Myra. She had yoga pants in one hand and a sports bra in the other. "I don't know what I am," Kat confessed. Then she let out the other part of her secret. "Michael and I broke up."

Myra stilled, but she didn't gasp or lecture. She simply nodded.

"A few weeks ago. I broke up with him," Kat added. "When he proposed, I wasn't a hundred percent certain I wanted to say yes. I was more like . . . I don't know . . . eighty percent? Maybe seventy percent?" Kat rolled the sports bra in her hand. "But Michael is a really great guy. He's a catch. I thought I could grow to be a hundred percent. But it just wasn't happening, and I freaked out."

Myra scooted close to Kat. She put a hand on her knee. "Sweetie, you deserve to be a hundred percent certain of the man you choose to marry. Nothing less. And definitely not seventy percent certain."

Kat put her hand on top of Myra's, sad that she hadn't seen much of her cousin in the past five years.

"Have you told anyone else?" Myra asked.

"No."

"How come?"

"I don't want to disappoint anyone. And I don't want to take any attention away from Jesse and Hazel. I guess I thought it would be easier to wait until after the wedding to tell Mom and Dad. And everyone."

"You're not going to disappoint anyone because you made a hard decision." Myra squeezed Kat's hand. "But your secret is safe with me."

"Thanks." Kat reached over and hugged Myra. "And thanks for listening."

"Anytime," Myra said, close to Kat's ear. She pulled back. "But we better get downstairs before my mom sends out a search team. You know how serious mom and Aunt Joyce are about their pie making. They've got an assembly line going on down there. You and I are on apple-slicing duty."

Kat grinned, despite her jumbled brain. "I'll meet you down there. Just need to change."

Myra stood from the bed and walked to the door. "But later, you better tell me the *whole* story about you and Creed and your dip in the lake. The *long* version." Myra stood with her hand on the doorknob, awaiting Kat's reply.

Kat shook her head and chuckled. "There's nothing more to tell."

"Mmmm hmmm," Myra sang and headed out the door with a wink.

Kat sat on the bed for another minute, analyzing the time she'd spent with Creed today. She'd easily fallen into a comfortable space with him, like she'd dropped into a time warp and went back a decade, or two. She considered how much she'd wanted to kiss him in the fleeting seconds she was pressed to his chest, searching his knowing eyes. There was so much between them. Good and bad. They were complicated, and Kat wondered what would happen if she exposed her lie to Creed. Would he be understanding, like Myra? Excited? Disgusted? Would she feel better after telling him the truth? Or worse?

Kat got up from the bed. She pulled off Creed's sweatshirt and replaced his clothes with her own. Still, she couldn't get him off her mind. Creed Sheridan had always owned space in her head, but she'd closed that door years ago. She'd locked it and thrown away the key. Now somehow her brain was taunting her, asking her to open the door and peek inside. How was it that Creed still had a hold on her heart?

The next morning brought a flurry of frustrations, all before eight o'clock. Kat couldn't sleep and ended up on the living room couch, tossing and turning. When the sun finally rose, Kat was tired and anxious but laced up her tennis shoes. She went for a good, long run, mulling through her problems as she pounded down country roads. And it was a good thing she'd started her morning like that, because as soon as she got back to the house, she was forced to take on the enigma that was her boss.

Instead of calling Kat to talk about what had conspired yesterday, Wendy set up a group video conference call at seven-thirty sharp. That didn't surprise Kat. Wendy liked to speak her mind in front of a crowd, especially when she thought she was right.

With her laptop situated on the bedroom dresser, Kat stood and stared at the screen. She'd washed the sweat off her face and slicked her hair back into a bun before throwing a polo shirt on top of her running gear. A full conference room stared back at her. Wendy was at the head of the long, glossy table. She was surrounded by product managers, the head of marketing, and their division's director. She'd brought in the big guns for whatever she was about to say.

"Katherine, as you know, I talked with the buyer from *Midwest Farm and Home* yesterday," Wendy started. "Since you're on vacation, I wanted to make sure I touched base with him concerning the meeting next week, to make sure there weren't any loose ends that needed to be addressed before then."

Kat nodded, thinking it was unbelievably annoying that Wendy thought it necessary to reach out to a client because Kat was *on vacation*, yet she had no trouble lining up video conference calls or blasting her with emails during her "time off."

"While I was talking with the buyer," Wendy continued, her tone condescending, "I mentioned our newest line of appliances and he said you'd never even mentioned them to him. Why is that?"

"Are you referring to the *Super Deluxe* appliances?" Kat asked. Wendy gave an abrupt nod. "I wasn't planning on presenting those specific items to that client because I don't feel like they're a good fit for their stores."

Wendy glanced around the table, looking shocked and offended. "Are you saying you aren't working to sell the new line our team has been working so hard to engineer? The appliances that have already won multiple awards for their innovation?" She raised her hands like she was dumbfounded.

"No, that's not what I'm saying." Kat knew her face was the size of a billboard on the screen in the conference room. She hoped that emphasized the annoyance in her eyes. "I am saying that the *Super Deluxe* line is not an appropriate match for this particular client. I've been working hard to get our new line into high-end retail chains, but *Midwest Farm and Home* is a farm store that prides itself on economically priced, quality products. Their customer will respond best to our opening price point, basic appliance line. I wasn't planning on presenting the *Super Deluxe* line because I don't think it will fit their store or their customer, and I only want to sell products that I know will fit my clients' needs. I'm not going to sell them products that will sit on their shelves and not sell. That doesn't help anyone. Not them. Not us."

"Well, that's not how Mr. Buxton saw it," Wendy chided, referring to the buyer she'd talked with yesterday. "As soon as I told him about the *Super Deluxe* appliances, he couldn't believe that you hadn't informed him of them sooner. He was appalled and decided to cancel our meeting because he didn't think you had his company's best interest in mind." Wendy raised her chin, waiting for Kat's response.

Had Kat really read that client wrong? After all her market research and conversations with the buyer? Had she totally missed the mark when deciding what products to present to him?

Wendy took advantage of Kat's momentary loss of words. "I suggest you reevaluate your presentation. Before Monday, I'd like to see a new presentation, focused on the *Super Deluxe* line, and I will reach out to Mr. Buxton to see if I can change his mind about reinstating next week's meeting."

Kat wanted to debate Wendy's request, but was also taken aback about what her boss had just said. It didn't align with any of Kat's previous conversations with Mr. Buxton.

"I'd like to give Mr. Buxton a call to make sure—" Kat started.

Wendy cut her off. "No need. I will call him today since we had such a great conversation yesterday. I think that's best. You start working on a revised presentation, and we'll touch base on Monday." Wendy reached for the remote that controlled the electronics in the conference room. "I've got another meeting starting in one minute. Have a good day, Katherine." With a tight smile, Wendy pressed a button on the remote and the video call went black.

Kat let out a pressurized groan, and her hands turned into fists. Wendy was the worst boss ever. The worst listener ever. When Wendy thought she was right, nothing else mattered. Frustrated, Kat paced between the dresser and the twin beds, vowing that she would be the opposite of Wendy if she got the promotion to national sales manager. Kat would work with the sales team instead of bullying them in one direction or the other. Kat would be respectful and open to everyone's ideas. She wouldn't pigeonhole anyone to what she thought was right.

"Ugh," Kat breathed and yanked off her polo, replacing it with her sweaty sweatshirt. She was going to need two runs this morning.

CHAPTER THIRTEEN

Creed knelt on the concrete floor of Gene's shop and rubbed the stain-soaked rag over the wooden chest. He made one last swipe before stepping back to inspect his work. Oak boards, antiqued hinges, a light coat of stain just to bring out the wood grain. The hope chest Creed had built for Jesse and Hazel's wedding present was almost complete. The only thing left to do was burn their names and wedding date into the underside of the hinged lid. He'd get that done yet today, before he left for the rodeo in Sugar Springs.

Ready to wrap up for now, Creed slid a few boxes in front of the hope chest, hiding it just in case Jesse wandered into the shop. So far, Creed had kept his gift a secret and only had to do so for a few more days. After pushing the boxes into place, Creed glanced out the open garage door. From the shop, he had a good view of the barn and the back of Gene and Joyce's house. The barn was quiet. Horses grazed in the fields. He and Evan had fed the horses early this morning, as the sun rose. Most of his days started that way. He helped the Westons whenever he could. Gene insisted on trying to pay him, but Creed wouldn't take a penny. Gene and Joyce had done plenty for him, to say the least. They'd steered him off the wrong path more times than he could count. Besides, he often reminded Gene that he got paid in shop space for his woodworking projects. Joyce also never let him go hungry. In Creed's eyes, a home-cooked meal was a currency more valuable than cash.

Stepping out of the building filled with tools, wood projects, and a tractor, Creed caught another sign of life. Kat was jogging past the barn. She stopped and began to stretch, and Creed figured she'd been running on the lake path. He turned back into the shop, counting how many days he had left until she went back to Chicago. *Four.* He wanted more time but knew that'd only put a bigger strain on his heart. And he wasn't sure how he was going to react when her fiancé came to town. Could he even take that visual? Seeing her happy with the man that had won her heart?

It might break him, but he wouldn't let anyone know it.

Creed cleaned his corner of the shop, busying himself by organizing tools, washing paint brushes, and folding drop cloths. When he heard a truck start just outside the shop, he stilled. Then his stomach dropped. The shop was a few hundred feet from the house. The only vehicle parked close to the shop was his dad's truck. It had been there since Creed and Kat had carried Rick out of *The Silver Saddle*.

Creed walked outside quickly. Sure enough, his dad was sitting in the truck. How had he gotten here?

Creed approached the truck, trying not to overreact. "Hey, I don't think that's a good idea."

Rick stared at him through the rolled-down window. His eyes were red, like he hadn't slept. Or, like he'd barreled through a pint of whiskey. "You don't get to tell me what to do with my truck."

"Not trying to tell you what to do." Creed caught the stench of liquor on Rick's breath. "Just trying to keep you from hurting yourself. Or someone else."

Rick tightened his grip on the steering wheel. "Why are you always in my business?"

He was *not* in Rick's business. They'd never been close. Ever since Creed came to live with Rick when he was fourteen, they'd simply existed in each other's lives. If anything, Creed had tried to stay out of Rick's business. Life was easier that way.

"Can I have the keys?" Creed raised his hand, knowing this was going to escalate. He was not in the mood for a wrestling match. He thought he'd grabbed the spare key out of Rick's trailer. Apparently, there was another. "I'll give you a ride home."

"What do you want from me?" Rick spat. He didn't offer up the key.

Nothing. I don't want anything from you. "I want you to go to an AA meeting. To get back on track. We all slip up. It happens."

"Slip up?" Rick laughed like Creed had just cracked a joke. "This is my life. This is how it is. You don't even know."

That almost made Creed laugh. Not because it was funny. Because it was so far from the truth. Creed had struggled with drinking ever since he was a teenager. Both his parents had addiction issues, and Creed thought that was normal until the Westons entered his life. In addition to showing him that alcohol wasn't part of the food triangle, Gene and Joyce showed him that family could be dependable, stable, and forgiving. Among many other things. Up until then, Creed hadn't realized he was following in his parents' footsteps, one stumbling step at a time. And it still took him many years before that lesson fully sank into his bones.

"I've relapsed. You know that." It pained Creed to remember, but he'd gotten behind the wheel drunk too. He'd crashed his truck and thanked the Lord every day that he'd only injured a fence. He knew how tempting it was to have a sip. He'd been on a roller coaster of drunk and sober through his twenties. Now he'd been sober for six years and was determined never to turn back to alcohol. That still didn't make it easy. "I want you to get help."

"I don't need help." Rick slammed the truck into gear, and Creed knew this wasn't going to end well. If his dad wasn't in a place where he could admit that he needed help, Creed was going to have a hard time convincing him to get it.

"Don't do this." Creed grabbed hold of the door and tried opening it. It was locked, so he pushed through the open window, battling Rick's flailing arm and swearing mouth. Creed tossed his arm across Rick's chest and grabbed for the key or gear shift, but Rick stepped on the gas and sent the truck backwards. Creed stumbled with it, and the truck slammed into something before Creed could stop it. The jolt forced Creed to stagger out the window. As he got his footing, Creed was sickened that Rick had managed to hit something, but the sickening feeling rushed away when he saw what he'd hit.

Creed's black Chevy was directly behind Rick's truck. The metal grill guard across the front pressed against Rick's tailgate, keeping the smaller truck from going anywhere.

Kat was driving Creed's truck.

"You okay?" she called out the window, her eyes flicking to Creed's. His truck rumbled like she'd touched the gas, threatening to push Rick's truck if needed.

Creed nodded and raised his hand, letting Kat know to stay put.

He turned back to Rick, knowing the front of Rick's truck faced a few big oak trees. Kat had him cornered.

Creed stepped toward the vehicle again. "Rick, you can't keep on like this. This is no way to live."

Rick groaned and squeezed his eyes shut in anger. He slammed his hand on the steering wheel and the horn blasted. He stayed in that position like he'd been tethered there, but as the seconds clicked by, his head slowly tipped forward until it hung. "I don't have a choice." Rick's words weren't loud, but they were clear, even over the rumbling diesel engine.

"You have a choice. We all have choices in life." The words reverberated through Creed, and he knew he had a choice here too. He'd been hurt plenty by Rick and knew it would be easier to turn his back on him. But life had taught Creed that the easy road wasn't always the one worth taking. "Let me help you. Come with me to an AA meeting. There's one at noon."

Rick winced. He didn't look at Creed, but after a grueling silence, Rick reached forward. He put his truck in park and took the key out of the ignition.

He handed the key to Creed.

CHAPTER FOURTEEN

Kat took a hot shower and threw on her favorite fleece sweatshirt—the one with the cowl neck that draped her like a scarf. She went downstairs, got a fresh cup of coffee, and sat at the kitchen table to sip and stare out into the backyard. Joyce and Judy chatted in the kitchen as they put the finishing touches on a crockpot of chili for supper tonight, but Kat didn't hear much of what they said. Images of what had happened this morning shot through her head. The work stuff had frustrated her, but it was miniscule compared to the incident with Rick.

Kat had just finished up her second run when she spotted Rick. He was walking down the driveway, and her heart had jumped into her throat, knowing exactly where he was going. She had immediately looked for Creed. His truck was parked at the front of the barn, but a swift jog down the barn aisle had told Kat that he wasn't there. And when Kat had heard Rick's truck start, she knew she needed to act quickly. Else he'd drive off, probably drunk.

Wanting to prevent that, Kat had fired up Creed's truck and rolled through the backyard toward Rick. She'd dialed Creed but threw her phone down when she saw Creed come out of the shop and approach Rick's truck. As she closed in, the two men were talking, but Kat knew how a conversation with Rick could quickly escalate. So when Rick's truck jumped into reverse, Kat made a split-second decision. She accelerated and came in behind him. Both trucks collided with a hard thud, and she kept her foot on the gas, blocking Rick from escaping.

"You want some more coffee, sweetie?" Joyce asked, already walking toward her with the pot.

Kat gave her a soft smile and raised her mug. "Thanks, Mom." As Joyce filled it, Kat stared at her kind, selfless mother. Her eyes welled up. She was beyond grateful for the parents she had. Not everyone was as lucky. "I love you."

"Oh, sweetness," Joyce cooed. She cupped Kat's cheek. "I love you most." She headed back to the kitchen. "It's so good to have you home."

"It's good to be here." Kat took a sip of the steaming coffee and glanced outside, letting gratitude settle in her chest. In the closest pasture, a few colts were playing, and their shenanigans grabbed Kat's attention. The colts kicked their heels up and raced by two older horses that were lazily grazing. Kat's sight fell on the black-and-white gelding. Her heart stirred, and she rose from the table. Heading to the kitchen counter, she plucked an apple from the fruit basket.

"You hungry?" Joyce and Judy asked at the same time.

"No," Kat replied. "I'm going to see Diesel."

Both women turned, obviously not expecting that answer.

Joyce recovered the quickest. "You better take two apples." She grabbed another and handed it to Kat. "If Chico sees you feeding Diesel, you know he's going to want one too."

Kat took the second apple. Joyce gave Kat's arm a rub before turning back to the chili. Her mom knew exactly how big of a step Kat was about to take.

Outside, Kat balanced the apples in one crooked arm. Carrying her coffee mug with her free hand, she took a few more sips as she walked across the backyard. When she reached the pasture, Kat set her mug on top of a fence post and shimmied through the boards. Diesel was happily grazing, unaware of her presence, and she was a bundle of nerves. Would Diesel ignore her like she'd been doing to him?

Kat whistled.

Diesel's head rose from the grass. He stopped chewing, like he'd heard something unusual. She called his name. This time Diesel's blazed face turned toward her. He took a step. Then he paused. For a second, Kat thought he was going to go back to grazing. Instead, he hopped into an energetic canter and soared across the pasture, straight to her.

His bountiful stride and eager eyes captured Kat. Memories rushed back to her. The snowy night Diesel was born. His spindly legs and baby-fuzz mane. How Kat had slept next to his mother's stall for a week, not wanting to miss his birth. The trail rides and rodeos he'd happily hauled her around at. The time he'd injured his leg and Kat had sold her car to pay for the vet bills. The bareback rides and sweet nickers. The endless days spent at the barn with her family and this horse.

Diesel slowed and stopped in front of her. He nickered.

"Hi, baby," she said, feeling choked. He raised his muzzle, and Kat blew a breath into his nostrils, hoping he remembered her scent.

He nuzzled her cheek, shoulder, and chest, making sure she was real. Kat raised her hand and stroked his white blaze. She threaded her fingers through his forelock and closed her eyes as she placed a kiss on his whiskered muzzle. He smelled the same. Like carefree youth.

"Can you forgive me?" She didn't know why it had taken her so long to come back to him. Sarah's death wasn't Diesel's fault. Kat knew that. She had never blamed him. She also knew Sarah would never have wanted Kat to give up her love of horses. "I've missed you. So much." She offered Diesel an apple. He nuzzled it and bit off exactly half, as he'd always done.

After Sarah's death, Kat had kept her distance from Diesel, the barn, and all the horses because it was too painful to relive what happened to her sister. But had her distance morphed into a punishment—for herself? Because of the guilt she carried from that night?

Diesel took the other half of the apple, drooling apple-slobber on her hand.

"Is that good?" Kat scratched his neck and chest, finding all the places she knew he loved. Then she leaned against him, burying her face in his black mane, and vowed to spend as much time with Diesel as she could while she was home. He deserved her love. She deserved to heal. And being here with her horse was one step closer to mending her heart.

Kat offered Diesel the second apple. "Don't tell Chico."

An hour later, Kat sat on top of the fence, watching the horses graze, finding peace again in their presence. She'd brushed Diesel from head to hoof, taking her time pampering him as he grazed in the pasture. She'd curried his whole body, rubbing slow circles through his coat. She'd brushed every tangle out of his tail. She braided his mane. She'd even groomed Chico when the sorrel horse curiously wandered over to see what all the fuss was about.

When Creed's truck rumbled down the driveway toward the barn, Kat hopped off the fence and started to pick up the arsenal of grooming tools she had scattered in the grass. As she gathered brushes, Creed slowed and stopped his truck along the fence. He rolled down the window. Kat gave him a wave.

"What ya doing?" He looked apprehensive.

"Brushing Diesel." Kat smiled. "And you were right. He remembered me."

Apprehension slid from Creed's face like she'd just told him the first good news he'd heard in a long time. "I knew he would."

Kat walked toward the truck with an armful of brushes. "How'd the meeting go?" she asked, hoping Rick hadn't flaked on the AA meeting. Or caused a scene. Kat had offered to go with Creed and Rick to the meeting, feeling protective of Creed, but Creed had declined her offer. She told herself not to worry. Creed could handle his dad without her. Still, she couldn't help the strong urge she had to be his backup.

Creed laid his arm across the open window. "Actually, it went good. Rick sat through the meeting. Didn't want to speak, but something must've resonated with him, because after the meeting, he called the detox at St. Mary's Hospital and checked himself in. I dropped him off."

Kat's eyes widened. "Really? Wow. I wasn't expecting that. I was just hoping he didn't cause a mess for you at the meeting. That's really good."

"Yeah, I think so."

Kat thought of how Creed had talked his dad into giving up the truck keys. In the past, confrontation between Creed and Rick would end in an explosive fight or with Creed slinking away. Today had been neither. "You did a really great job of keeping calm and getting his keys," Kat said. "I couldn't have done that. You kept your cool. I wanted to yell every swear word in my vocabulary at him." She still did.

"It helped that he couldn't go anywhere." Creed was staring at her like she'd roped the moon.

Kat grinned back. "What are you up to now? Cleaning stalls?" It'd been a long time since she mucked out a stall. Too long. Maybe they could do it together?

"Nah. The stalls are all cleaned. Evan and I did them this morning. I'm going to finish up a woodworking project in the shop. Then I'm off to a rodeo in Sugar Springs."

"A rodeo? Tonight?"

Creed nodded. "I'm close to qualifying for the National Finals Rodeo and can't really miss it."

Kat rolled her teeth over her bottom lip. It had also been forever since she'd been to a rodeo. "Do you want company?"

"You want to go with me to the rodeo?" he asked, looking like she'd asked him if she could enter his truck in a demolition derby. Though she'd already done that today.

She gave him a shrug. "I don't have anything else to do tonight. We aren't setting up for the groom's supper until the morning." Then she felt awkward for asking. "It's fine, though, if you don't want me to tag along. I didn't mean to—"

Creed interrupted her. "I'll pick you up in a half hour."

Her fingers tightened around the curry comb in her hand. "Okay. See you then."

As Creed drove off toward the shop, Kat walked to the barn. She put the brushes back in the tack room and then headed to the house to clean up. There were a few things she wanted to do before she went to the rodeo with Creed. First, she needed to find her cowboy boots.

Second, she wanted to take off her engagement ring.

CHAPTER FIFTEEN

Kat tugged her fleece sleeves down, covering most of her bare hands. A crisp autumn chill hung in the air, but she wasn't cold. Inside Creed's truck, the cab was warm. Toasty. Still, Kat didn't want to spotlight her lack of jewelry. She'd tell Creed the truth tonight—about her broken engagement. She just wasn't sure when or how. And she wasn't ready to start that conversation right now.

"How'd you like driving *The Cowboy Cadillac?*" Creed asked as they careened down quiet country roads lined with tilled farm fields and rolling hills. "It's been a long time since you've driven her."

Kat had playfully given his truck that nickname—*The Cowboy Cadillac*—the first year he got it. Which now almost twenty years ago. "She drives just like I remember." Kat gave Creed a slight smile. "Like a tank."

Creed patted the dashboard affectionately. "This tank hasn't let me down yet."

"Never wanted to trade her in for something new and shiny?" she teased.

Creed slid her a look. "Trade her in? Not going to happen. Once you find something you love," his voice faltered, "there's no sense in looking elsewhere."

Kat froze. Her brain short-circuited. Was she being hyper-sensitive or was he talking about more than his truck?

Creed shot her his Hollywood smile. "I'll get another truck eventually," he said. "But I'll never get rid of *The Cowboy Cadillac*. Just can't. We've been through too much together."

Kat eyed Creed and brushed away her thoughts. He was talking about his truck. Not her. "I hope there wasn't any damage to the front end." She'd come in hot when rear-ending Rick's truck, not having time to consider the damage it would cause to Creed's vehicle.

"Nah, she's a tough old bird. And the grill across the front is practically bulletproof. A little fender bender can't hurt her."

"Good."

"By the way, thank you." The playfulness was gone from Creed's voice. "I wouldn't have gotten through to Rick if you hadn't stopped him."

Kat crossed her arms over her stomach, suddenly not sure what to do with them. "It was nothing. Glad I could help." The radio hummed softly, and Kat wanted to ease the pressure rising in the cab. She reached for the radio knobs. "Mind if I change the station?"

"Go for it." Creed adjusted his visor to shade the late-afternoon sun from his eyes.

Kat twisted the radio knob, scanning for her favorite station. She gave a little gasp when she found it, craving some old-school country tunes. "They play the best music." Turning the volume up, Kat sat back and bobbed her head to a song she hadn't heard since she was little.

"This *is* a good one." Creed began tapping his thumb on the steering wheel.

The song was just what they needed. For a few minutes, they both swayed to strumming guitars and a soulful harmony. Kat hummed along, staring through the windshield as they rolled along a familiar country road. But when the next song started, Kat and Creed looked at each other like lightning had struck. In the first three cords, Kat recognized the song that had defined the summer of her senior year—the summer Kat and Creed had spent lost in each other.

Summer Love, Forever on my Mind.

They'd blasted this song on the sandbar from a little silver radio that ran off batteries and a tall antenna. The lyrics had sung out of loudspeakers as Creed burst from chutes on bulls. Kat had even made a mixtape for Creed. It was the first song on the tape and had been the start of many teenage makeout sessions.

It wasn't a slow, sappy song. The beat was fast. The words captured how Creed and Kat had been together as teenagers—spellbound and crazy in love.

Now, nearly twenty years later, the song still had the power to transport her back in time. On one hand, Kat wanted to sing along. On the other, she thought about opening the door and jumping from the moving vehicle. Listening to the song right now was like playing a movie that highlighted every good and bad time they'd gone through together.

"We don't have to listen to—" Kat reached for the radio knob.

Creed caught her hand. He didn't speak, but his eyes said a whole lot. Kat dropped her hand to the seat.

The song continued, filling the cab, and when Creed's steel-toed boot started tapping, Kat's eyes shot to his foot. By the second verse, Creed was humming. Then singing. He got progressively louder, and Kat couldn't take her eyes off him. She blinked. She smiled. Then she laughed. When he returned her laugh, Kat couldn't believe it, but she started singing with him. By the middle of the song, they were soaring down the two-lane road, singing at the top of their lungs. Neither of them could keep a tune, but the harmony was flawless.

When the song came to an end, Kat sighed and slouched against the seat, feeling like a weight had been lifted from her shoulders.

"Now, *that* was a good song." Kat said.

"The best." Creed winked at her.

When the next song started, they joined in without missing a beat.

Creed pulled into the Sugar Springs Fairgrounds and drove around to the back lot, where the rodeo contestants parked and camped. The lot was a mowed field full of horse trailers, campers, and trucks. A few riders moseyed through on their horses. Creed backed into a circle of trucks and trailers, parking so that his tailgate faced a campfire surrounded by empty lawn chairs.

"Bareback broncs won't start until after eight. Want to get something to eat at the fair?" Creed asked.

Kat glanced at the clock on the dash. It was just past five. They had a few hours to kill. "Yes, please. It's been *forever* since I've had fair food."

"Gyros and deep-fried candy bars?" Creed gave her a knowing glance.

Kat placed her hand on her chest and made a sound as if she hadn't eaten in weeks. "Oh, you know the way to a girl's heart."

"I try." Creed got out of the truck. He walked around the front and was at her door as she opened it. He offered a hand to help her out. It was a big step to the ground, so Kat took his hand and climbed down.

When her boots hit the grass, Kat looked up at Creed. "Want to split an order of cheese curds too?" Kat nearly drooled at her own question, but Creed didn't seem as entranced by the mention of cheese curds. His eyes were glued to their intertwined hands, and the blood rushed from Kat's face. She knew what he was looking at.

"You're not wearing your ring." His dark-green eyes clicked back to hers.

The conversation she'd been dreading was going to happen now. Kat searched for words. She wanted to tell Creed a lot of things but wasn't sure how to package them into an explanation that made sense. She wasn't engaged. Not anymore. She'd been wearing the ring in a feeble attempt to protect her heart. No matter how crazy that sounded, it was true. She'd never forgotten how Creed had made her feel. She'd been chasing that feeling ever since they parted, but she'd never been able to replicate it.

"Creed, I wanted to tell you—" Kat's eyes shifted down, away from his. Guilt riddled her, but her explanation was cut off when a woman came out of the camper next to Creed's truck.

"Kat?" the woman screeched.

Kat turned, her hand falling from Creed's. She found a very pregnant woman waddling toward her. "Hannah?"

Hannah's arms stretched out, a huge grin on her face. "Oh, my goodness! Where'd you come from?" She made it sound like Kat had just emerged from a secret hiding spot.

"Hey," Kat tried to get her head out of the conversation she needed to have with Creed. Emotions flipped through her, but she batted them away to greet a friend she hadn't seen in at least ten years. "Wow, look at you."

Kat and Hannah hugged. They knew each other from the rodeo circuit, back when Kat used to compete. Hannah lived in North Dakota, but they used to run barrels at many of the same events.

Kat pulled back and looked at Hannah's basketball belly. "Congratulations!"

Hannah placed both hands on her stomach. "Thank you." She beamed. "Quinn and I got married."

"Quinn the rodeo clown?" Kat asked.

"Yep, he's my clown now." Hannah smiled. "I'm due in a week, but we had one more rodeo to hit. Quinn's in the arena now, but I've got four little ones sleeping in the camper."

Kat's mouth fell open. "Four?"

Hannah rubbed her belly. "Yep, this is baby number five for us."

"Oh, wow." Kat remembered Hannah in her early twenties, going from rodeo to rodeo with her beautiful quarter horse, Frenchie. Hannah and Frenchie were a hard team to beat. Somehow Kat didn't picture Hannah settled down with a trailer full of babies. She figured she'd have a trailer full of horses.

"Hannah and Quinn have their hands full," Creed said, joining Kat at her side, acting like nothing had just happened between the two of them. "They've made a beautiful family."

"Aw, aren't you just the cutest?" Hannah reached out and patted Creed on the arm. "It'd happen for you too if you'd just find the right girl." She winked, playfully, meaning no harm, but her comment hit home for Kat. After Kat left for college, Creed had hopped through the dating scene the same way he flitted from rodeo to rodeo. And it seemed like he was still on the same path. Kat wasn't sure he'd ever settle down.

"Last time I heard you were living in Chicago. Still there?" Hannah asked Kat.

"Yep. Just in town for Jesse's wedding," Kat replied as two more old friends approached from the circle of trucks and trailers—Ellie and Destin. Like Kat and Hannah, Ellie had also grown up competing in barrel racing. Destin roped. Kat had heard they'd gotten married a few years ago.

"Look who's here!" Hannah announced to the newcomers.

Ellie and Destin raced in for hugs, and by the time they'd all caught up on the past decade, Kat's stomach was rumbling. Creed must've heard it.

"We were going to find some food," Creed said to the group.

"Mind if we join you?" Ellie asked, grabbing hold of Destin's arm. "I've got a hankering for a corn dog."

Hannah practically growled. "That sounds *so* good."

"We'll bring you back two corn dogs," Creed said to Hannah. "Want anything else?"

"Maybe a funnel cake?" Hannah raised her eyebrows innocently.

"You're going to give that baby diabetes," Ellie laughed.

"He's hungry!" Hannah playfully slapped her friend's shoulder. "Besides, I can treat myself every now and then."

"Hey, don't taunt the pregnant lady," Destin chided. "Of course, we'll get you a funnel cake."

"He's just saying that so he can share it with me," Hannah winked at Destin. He shrugged like he'd been caught.

Ellie and Destin walked with Creed and Kat, chatting as they passed bull pens and the warm-up arena. When they entered the area packed with food trucks and carnival rides, Kat tried to focus on the moment, instead of what she needed to get off her chest. She could explain her lack of an engagement ring on their drive home, in private. Besides, Creed was being his normal, jokey self. Maybe he wasn't concerned about her disappearing ring?

They each got their chosen fried foods and stood in a circle to gobble them up. As Kat ate her gyro, Destin and

Ellie rehashed a few old stories and updated Kat on all that had changed with their circle of rodeo friends. When Creed offered up the paper bowl of cheese curds they were sharing, Kat plucked the biggest from the pile and plopped the batter-covered curd into her mouth. The crispy batter and warm, gooey cheese melted together in her mouth. Her eyes rolled back in her head.

"There's not a restaurant in Chicago that can make a better cheese curd," she admitted, licking grease from her fingers. "Unreal."

Creed was watching her, amused. "The rodeo crew knows how to do fried food right."

She snatched another curd. "Aren't you going to help me eat these?" Creed had only eaten a few.

"Nah, I've had my fill. Don't want to regurgitate cheese and grease when I get tossed from a bronc in a few hours," he said.

Kat wrinkled her nose at that visual.

"What horse did you draw?" Destin asked.

"Dark Descent," Creed replied with an easy tone.

Destin grunted like Creed was about to hop on a dragon.

Kat looked back and forth between Destin and Creed. "Is that not a good draw?"

Creed tipped his head. "It's good if I can keep up with him."

"He's dirty, though," Ellie said, referring to the horse. "Never does the same thing twice out of the chute and bucks like a maniac."

"Makes it hard to get a good score," Creed added. "But I'm pretty dirty too. I'm up for the challenge."

Kat knew Creed was always up for the challenge. When it came to rodeo, he didn't acknowledge fear. Was that a little crazy? Yes, but Kat had always known that was also his secret weapon. Not being afraid of what was to come was half the battle of overcoming it. Kat wished she had that superpower.

"Hey, since we're here," Ellie said. "Can we play some carnival games?" She looked excited by this idea. Destin did not.

"Which game do you want to lose money on?" Destin sighed.

Kat chuckled at his pessimism. "What? You're not going to win a prize for your beautiful bride?"

Ellie batted her eyelashes dramatically at Destin. "How about the rope ladders? They have the cutest teddy bears."

"That game is so rigged," Creed said.

"You should both do it," Kat said to Destin and Creed. "Come on, it's not that hard. Win us each teddy bears." Kat took the tray of curds from Creed, freeing up his hands.

He cocked his head at her. "You want a teddy bear?" He seemed intrigued by this.

She shrugged. "I dare you."

The three words fell out of her mouth easily, but Kat knew they'd motivate Creed. Growing up, Kat had watched Jesse, Evan, and Creed dare each other to do the stupidest things—eat jalapeños, take arctic plunges into the lake, jump four-wheelers, talk to girls. Creed was the only one she'd never seen back down from a dare. Eventually, Kat had taken her brothers' cues and often dared Creed as well—to race her on Diesel, do a backflip off the dock . . . *to kiss her.* Their first kiss had been next to a campfire on the sandbar, instigated by her dare. That dare had propelled her out of a crush and into her first love.

"You *dare* me to win you a teddy bear?" Creed asked.

"I dare you."

There was a flash of recognition on Creed's face. Then he turned to Destin. "Come on. Let's win these ladies some teddy bears."

CHAPTER SIXTEEN

It took Creed three tries to climb the wobbly rope ladder, but he finally rang the bell and won a teddy bear for Kat. She beamed when he handed it to her, and Creed considered winning her a second bear. Or a third. Instead, they cheered on Destin, who could've bought a truckload of stuffed animals with the money he spent defeating the carnival game for Ellie.

When both Kat and Ellie had bears, all four of them walked back to the trucks and trailers, where Creed grabbed his canvas duffel bag from his truck's backseat. The bag contained everything he needed for his ride.

"It's about time I get to the chutes," Creed said, slinging the bag over his shoulder and across his chest.

"I'll come with," Kat said, setting her teddy bear in the backseat of Creed's truck. "I'd like to watch some of the rodeo before you ride."

Creed reached around Kat, grabbing hold of the edge of the door, intending to shut it for her, but when she turned around, she spun right into his chest. Her hand fell to his arm, and a little gasp escaped her full lips. Creed called on his wavering self-control to keep his hands where they were. He wanted to take hold of her. Would he ever stop wanting Kat? Was he destined to be tortured forever?

She pressed her lips together. Her fingertips grazed his biceps, almost like she meant to linger there. Every muscle in Creed's back tightened.

"Did you get your teddy bear situated?" Creed asked, holding her stare, taking in her brown-sugar eyes and dark lashes.

Kat's cheeks went rosy. If nothing else, at least Creed knew her physical attraction to him was still there. He smirked, enjoying her flushed face.

Kat gave him a little push. "Better get your head in the game, cowboy."

That he did need to do.

"Let's go so we can get seats on the bleachers closest to the chutes," Ellie called from the campfire. "You ready?"

"Ready," Kat sang back and gave Creed one more look before joining Ellie.

What was that? Was she flirting with him?

Creed gave his head a shake and walked next to Destin toward the arena. The girls were right in front of them.

No more nonsense. You have a bronc to ride and money to earn.

It was time to concentrate on his job. Though Creed shouldn't be walking directly behind Kat if he wanted to get his head straight. She was wearing an old pair of Wranglers, and they hugged her in all the right places.

Creed kept his eyes up and focused on the arena, glad when they arrived at the chutes. He waved to Kat, Ellie, and Destin, and left them at the bleachers. They called out wishes of good luck as he climbed the stairs to the platform behind the chutes and joined the other competitors. Once he was on the platform, Creed set down his bag and started to prep for his ride. He pulled his yellow-fringed chaps out of his bag and buckled them around his waist. Zipping the leather chaps over his jeans, Creed ruminated over what he'd discovered earlier—that Kat wasn't wearing her engagement ring. At first, he figured she'd taken it off and had forgotten to put it back on, but when he'd asked her about it, the look on her face told him there was more to the story. Creed didn't know a lot about Michael, but he knew Kat deserved to be treated like a queen. If Michael had hurt Kat, Creed would straighten him out.

He slid into his protective vest, then worked his right hand into his worn leather glove and laced it up tight. As he did, Creed decided he'd ask Kat about Michael on the drive home. If there was something bothering her, he wanted her to confide in him, like she used to.

Determined to get to the root of it—later—Creed shoved his black cowboy hat on his head. Then he snatched up his rigging and cinch, flung them over his shoulder, and started his pre-ride ritual. Earbuds went into his ears, and Creed turned on the playlist he listened to before every ride. Electric guitars and pounding drums amped him up and filtered his thoughts. He stretched his muscles and jogged in place. This was exactly what he needed—a laser focus and, ultimately, the rush and release that came from the ride.

Thirty minutes later, Creed was ready for his challenge.

He walked toward the chute and eyed the dark-bay horse waiting for him. *Dark Descent* peered at Creed through the metal panel. The horse wasn't scared or mad. He was stock still, analyzing Creed, deciding what he might do to the man that dared to get on his back.

Creed knelt near the panels. "It's just you and me," he murmured to the horse. "We've each got a job to do for eight seconds."

Dark Descent kicked the back of the chute like he wanted Creed to know what he was in for.

Creed winked at the horse, appreciating his grit. Then he climbed up the panel and lowered himself into the chute. A handful of cowboys made last-minute preparations as Creed eased onto *Dark Descent's* wide, muscular back, making sure not to touch his boots or spurs to the horse's sides. The chute was a dangerous place, and Creed didn't want to startle the bronc before his ride. He'd seen plenty of broken bones caused by a rear or scramble in the chute.

As his butt settled on hide, Creed slid his gloved hand into the rigging that circled the bronc's ribcage. He crept his legs forward, in front of the horse's shoulders, ready to mark out. Putting his free hand in the air, Creed nodded, indicating he was ready.

A moment later, the chute flung open, and *Dark Descent* burst up and out, sailing into the arena. Music blared. The audience roared. But Creed was hyper-focused on his ride— so much so that the rest of the world fell away. All that mattered was predicting the jackhammer movements below him and making sure that he matched them.

Dark Descent lurched and kicked with all the dirt and grit Creed knew he had. He cracked Creed's torso like a whip. His cowboy hat soared off like a frisbee, and Creed clung to the bronc, using hard-earned muscle to stay put. He held tight through one tricky jolt after another, through each attempt to toss him. Every buck fueled Creed. Pain didn't register. The past didn't hurt. Sometimes Creed wished he got more than eight seconds. Here, atop a gritty horse, Creed truly felt weightless. It was the only place he felt like that.

When the whistle called, telling Creed his time was up, Creed grabbed hold of the rigging. He steadied his body until *Dark Descent* eased up on the bucking and moved into a rowdy run. Two pick-up men rode their horses toward Creed, and Creed yanked his gloved hand from the rigging, preparing to dismount. When the two riders surrounded the bronc, matching the horse's speed, Creed leaned over and reached for a pick-up man's waist, ready to grab hold and pull himself off *Dark Descent's* back. It was something he'd done a million times.

But *Dark Descent* had other ideas.

Before Creed had hold of the pick-up man, *Dark Descent* spun like a top, reversing his direction and peeling free of Creed. Creed instantly knew he was in trouble. He fell, inches from *Dark Descent's* hind end.

Before Creed hit the ground, legs and hooves whaled on him. The crowd collectively gasped, and Creed didn't even feel the dirt before his vision went black.

CHAPTER SEVENTEEN

Being at the rodeo with Creed had brought back so many memories. Every sight, sound, and smell reminded Kat of how much fun she used to have. She found herself wondering why she ever gave it up.

Then she watched Creed ride.

Kat was on her feet through his entire ride, her nerves and excitement coming out in jumps and yells. She screamed encouragement and clapped her hands through every impressive buck, amazed at Creed's strength and agility, knowing most men wouldn't make it past one of *Dark Descent's* thrashing kicks. The sight made her heart pound—for multiple reasons—and when the whistle blew, Kat threw her hands in the air. She hugged Ellie, knowing Creed would get a high score with the ride he'd just had. Then she turned back to the arena, expecting to see Creed hop to the ground and complete his signature fist-pump to the sky. Instead, she watched him get pummeled.

Kat's relief flipped to horror as Creed proceeded to get kicked in the back. The impact was enough to lift his body up and over the rump of the pick-up man's horse. Kat gasped as Creed tumbled to the ground. When he laid there in a heap, her stomach turned. She'd watched Creed take some nasty falls before, but he always got up on his own. This time he laid there like a rag doll.

The music stopped. The announcer said something to reassure the audience. EMTs rushed out into the arena, but Kat ran from the bleachers before they made it to Creed. She knew where the ambulance and medical tent sat, and she wasn't going to waste time getting there.

Dread filled Kat as she ran around the arena, barreling past food tents and zigzagging through unsuspecting bystanders who were happily eating corndogs and cotton candy. As she ran, Kat felt the cheese curds she'd shared with Creed threaten to come back up.

Please, Lord. Let him be okay.

"We're right behind you!" Ellie called, but Kat didn't look back.

When she rounded the backside of the arena, she spotted the white medical tent. The ambulance was parked beside it. As she ran toward the tent, four EMTs appeared from the arena. They were carrying a stretcher. Creed was on it.

Kat held her tongue, continuing to pray that Creed was okay. She felt a small pang of relief when she saw that his eyes were open. His gaze fell on her. He looked like he was in pain.

"Creed," Kat called. One of the EMTs stopped her.

"Hang on, ma'am," he warned, putting a hand up. "We need to check him over. Wait right here."

They hauled the stretcher into the tent, and Kat reluctantly stopped. Ellie and Destin joined her.

"He'll be okay," Ellie said. She took hold of Kat's arm, trying to reassure her, but Kat knew better. An image of her sister being hauled away on a stretcher suddenly consumed Kat's mind, and in that moment, she physically felt how fragile life was. Kat wanted to be by Creed's side. Now.

She shook free of Ellie's grasp and stepped into the tent, disregarding the warning to stay put.

The tent had just enough room for the stretcher, one other bed, a few plastic chairs, and medical supplies. The EMT who had told her to stay put immediately gave her an annoyed look.

"Ma'am, unless you're his wife, I'm going to need you to wait outside." The man pointed to the door as the other EMTs helped Creed out of his vest.

Kat opened her mouth to tell the EMTs that she was Mrs. Sheridan, or any other lie that got her to Creed, but Creed spoke first.

"I want her in here," he said. He took a seat on the bed. "If you're going to insist that you check me over, I want Kat with me."

The annoyed EMT pointed to the plastic chair. "Sit, please."

Kat sat stiffly and watched as the EMTs poked and prodded Creed, asking him questions as they went. Kat's fear had eased when Creed spoke. He sounded more grumpy than pained, but that didn't squelch the worry that had taken over her insides.

"Ma'am?" the EMT asked. Kat jerked.

"Yes?" Kat stood abruptly. An EMT handed Creed his vest. He shimmied into it gingerly.

"Are you able to drive your friend home?"

Kat nodded. "Yes, of course."

"Good, because I don't suggest that he drive tonight. Creed suffered a concussion, and I highly suggest he take it easy for a few days. And no rodeo for at least a month." Behind the EMT, Creed was grumbling, looking like he was ready to go. "If he shows signs of dizziness or confusion, I suggest going to see a doctor as soon as possible. Especially if there is vomiting or he loses consciousness again. For the next few days, make sure he drinks lots of water and takes pain medication as needed. Are you able to stay with him tonight?"

Kat was nodding with every instruction, but the last question caught her off guard. It must've done the same to Creed because he stopped his grumbling.

"Stay with him?" Kat repeated.

"Yes, someone should check on him every few hours tonight to make sure his symptoms aren't worsening. If they do, I'd suggest an ER visit."

Creed stood. "Thank you, but I'm fine."

The EMT gave Kat a look that disagreed with Creed's statement.

"I'll take care of him," Kat said to the EMT. "Thank you."

Creed left the tent, and Kat followed. Ellie and Destin were waiting outside.

"Hey, you okay?" Destin asked, concerned. "That didn't look good."

Ellie made a face like she agreed.

Creed waved his hand, making light of the situation. "No broken bones. I'm good to go."

"You had a concussion," Kat added. "I think we should get home so you can rest."

"I can get your bag from the chutes," Destin offered. "Meet you guys at the trucks?"

"Thanks, Destin," Kat replied, before Creed could retort.

"Want me to pick up your check too?" Destin asked Creed. "You got the high score. Won it with an eighty-five."

Creed rolled his shoulder like he was trying to work something out. "Nah, I'll pick it up."

Destin gave Creed a congratulatory pat on the arm and jogged off to grab his bag.

CHAPTER EIGHTEEN

Kat was driving Creed's truck for the second time that day. On the way back to Maple Bay, she focused on the road ahead of her—the yellow lines and approaching headlights—and tried to drown out the image of Creed lying in the arena dirt. She couldn't, so she tapped her fingers on the steering wheel and counted down the minutes until she finally parked Creed's truck on the dead-end road that faced his boat. When the rumbling of the engine stopped, Creed stirred in the backseat. Kat turned to look at him. He was sprawled out on the bench seat, blinking away sleep, using her teddy bear as a pillow.

Kat was glad he'd rested for the last part of the drive. "How are you feeling?"

Creed sat up and grimaced. "Like I got kicked in the back by a horse."

She shot him a frown. "Time for you to go to bed." She got out of the truck and opened the back door. Creed slid out, holding her teddy bear to his chest. He put a hand to his lower back like he was twice his age.

He handed the stuffed animal to Kat and rolled his shoulders as if trying to loosen something up. "I might have a *Dark Descent* hoof tattoo on my shoulder."

"You're lucky you don't have one on the back of your head," Kat said as they walked toward the dock.

Once inside the boat, Creed clicked on a lamp. "You don't have to stay. I heard what the EMT said. I'll go to the doctor if I get worse."

Kat stared at him, wondering if he could be any more stubborn. "If you heard what the EMT said, you'd know that someone has to check on you every few hours tonight. I can stay."

Sasquatch sauntered out of the bedroom. He circled Creed's feet and meowed a welcome. Creed bent down and ran a hand over the cat's orange body. "You miss me or you just out of food?" Sasquatch meowed again. "Both?" Creed opened a kitchen cabinet and pulled out a bag of cat food. He filled Sasquatch's bowl, put the bag back in the cupboard, and grabbed a jumbo-sized bottle of ibuprofen that sat next to the cat food. "Good thing I buy this in bulk." Creed popped a few pills into his mouth and swallowed them without water.

Kat took a glass out of a cupboard and filled it at the sink. "Drink, please." She watched as Creed downed the water. When he set the glass on the counter, Kat asked, "How many concussions have you had?"

He looked at her like she was challenging him. She was.

"How many?" she asked again.

"A few."

She tried to force some sense into Creed with her eyes. "How long are you going to keep this up?" There were so many other career paths he could take, outside of strapping himself to dynamite.

"Keep what up?"

"Riding broncs."

Creed stilled. The sound of Sasquatch crunching kibble filled the cabin. "Why would I give it up?"

"Because you can still walk away." Kat set the teddy bear Creed had won her on the counter. "It's dangerous, Creed. There's a good chance that one of these times you *won't* make it out of the arena, and I don't want to see that happen."

Creed's jaw tightened, and he scraped a hand through his blond hair, mussing it. "Why?"

Kat braced herself against his question. "What do you mean? I don't want to see you get hurt."

"And what do you suggest? That I give up rodeo? Rodeo is my life, Kat. It's my job. I can't just give it up."

"You don't have to get on a bronc or a bull." She paused, taking in his stiff posture. "You've been roping just as long. You're amazing at that, too. Why don't you focus on an area of rodeo where you're less likely to get hurt? Or focus on your woodworking? You could easily make a living off that." She threw a hand at his kitchen cabinets like she was trying to knock them over.

"Why do you care?" Creed asked. Sasquatch strolled into the bedroom like he didn't want to be part of this conversation.

"I care about *you*, Creed." The fact that she had to say it made her mad. Then it hurt her. This had once been a man she wanted to marry, someone she couldn't see her life without. Of course she cared if he put himself in a situation he might not come out of. Even if they weren't together, she cared about his well-being.

Creed shook his head. "I don't think you do." Then he turned and walked into his bedroom, leaving Kat with her mouth wide open, feeling like she'd just been dismissed.

She was *not* going to be dismissed.

Kat joined him in the bedroom, intending to correct him. "I do care about you, Creed. No matter what you think."

He was unbuttoning his collared shirt, revealing the T-shirt beneath. "You left me, Kat. You ran away and never looked back. How is that caring?"

Her heart twisted like he'd just grabbed it with his fist. That was how he remembered it? "I left because I couldn't handle what happened to Sarah. I told you that."

"You told me that five years later." He peeled off his collared shirt and threw it in the full hamper. "Ever since that night, I've beat myself up for what happened. For what I did. For how I could've done something, *anything* different. And I know you have too. We lost Sarah that night, but we didn't have to lose each other. That was *your* choice, Kat."

"It wasn't a choice," she said, dumbfounded. After Sarah passed, Kat's insides were stripped bare. She had nothing to give. She couldn't have loved Creed then, no matter what he'd said or done. "I didn't choose any of that. I was just trying to keep my head above water. I wasn't in a place where I could love you."

Creed swallowed and rolled his head back like she'd punched him under the chin. He briefly closed his eyes. When he opened them, his eyes were dark, pained. More so than when he was on the stretcher earlier today. "You never came back to me. I thought you would at some point. That we could talk it out. Instead, you found love with someone else."

Kat touched her thumb to her ring finger. She'd taken her ring off earlier today because she felt safe enough to do so. She no longer felt safe.

Creed pulled off his T-shirt and tossed it on the floor. Bare-chested, he said, "You might want to turn around." He unclipped his belt buckle and started to unbutton his jeans.

At the first hint of his underwear, Kat turned. She listened to him changing. His belt buckle jangled. Drawers opened and closed. Clothing shifted against skin. All the while, she tried to sift through her anger and hurt. She *had* tried to run away from Creed. He wasn't wrong about that. Yet here she was. Standing in his bedroom, being pushed and pulled in all kinds of directions and not knowing which way to go.

Kat put her head in her hands. She took a breath for courage and found her words. "I didn't find love," she admitted. Not looking Creed in the eye gave her the gumption to spill her secret. "Michael and I broke up a few weeks ago."

The room went still. *Silent.* Beyond silent.

"What'd you say?" Creed asked.

"I'm not in love. I'm not engaged." Blood pounded against her eardrums.

"I don't understand," Creed said, slowly pronouncing the words. "Why'd you tell me you were?"

I was protecting my heart from you.

"I was confused," Kat said. Then she corrected herself. "I am confused." She was more confused than ever.

Kat heard Creed move.

"What happened?" His voice vibrated against her back. "What'd he do?"

"Nothing." Michael hadn't done anything wrong. Still, Kat couldn't picture herself walking down the aisle with him, committing her life to him. "I . . . I just couldn't do it. I broke it off."

He wasn't you.

"Kat?" Creed's voice had closed in. He was just behind her. "Can you look at me?"

She didn't want to turn around. Could she look him in the eye and *not* fall into his arms? Being with Creed this week had brought back emotions she'd been suppressing for a long time. Feelings she'd thought—or hoped—had fizzled away. They hadn't. Now she was certain her feelings for him had been burning below the surface, waiting for the chance to take hold and rise up. If she turned around, was she setting herself up to take flame? To burn down to embers?

Closing her eyes, Kat said, "I left Maple Bay because I wanted a new life." She forced herself to open her eyes and turn around. Creed was an arm's length away. He'd changed into sweatpants and a clean, white T-shirt. His face was sullen, serious. "I thought if I left, I could make a new life that didn't include all the pain and guilt I felt after losing Sarah. I thought time and distance would heal the gaping wound I had in my heart."

His Adam's apple slid down his neck. "Did it?"

"No." She shook her head. *Still have a gaping wound.*

"You can't heal by forgetting," Creed said, and Kat pressed her lips together.

"I don't want to forget. It's just—" Tears pricked Kat's eyes. She was talking about Sarah and Creed in the same breath. "I think I've been so angry and disappointed in myself that I thought I didn't deserve to remember . . . to remember the good things." Kat let her gaze settle into Creed's emerald eyes. She tried to read his stoic face. She almost wished he'd crack a joke. Then she let her mouth say what her brain didn't want her to. "And you are one of those good things, Creed. I thought I could forget you. You didn't deserve that. You didn't deserve to be cut out of my life. I'm sorry I did that. I wish I could take it back. I wish—" Her words faltered, but her head continued shaking, back and forth.

Creed reached out. He cupped her jaw and cheek, stilling her head. His hand was warm, calloused. A few hours ago, it had kept him aboard a wild bronc. Now it was trying to settle her worries.

"I've never forgotten you," Creed whispered. "I can't."

His touch forced a current down her body. She remembered exactly what it felt like to be wrapped up in Creed. She'd never truly forgotten.

"I care about you," Kat said. "I never stopped, even when I wanted to. I want you to be happy. And safe."

Creed nodded slowly, like he was sorting through every word she'd just said. He brushed his thumb over her cheek.

His other hand rose. It slid over her neck. Her pulse hammered, and she wondered if Creed could feel it.

"I need to kiss you," he said, and stepped toward her like she'd pulled him.

His stare pinned her in place. She couldn't move. Kat watched as Creed inched closer and closer. She watched until their lips touched.

And the intensity of his kiss grew in waves. It was like nothing she'd ever felt. Not even with him. Creed's fingers slid into her hair. His lips explored hers with a need that melted through her, consuming her body and mind. Goosebumps turned to heat. Nerves crackled with electricity. Her heart pounded like a bass drum.

What is happening? What are we doing?

Kat reached out, putting her hands on his arms, steadying herself, not sure if her heart was about to break or overflow. Her fingers slid over skin and snuck beneath cotton sleeves. She dug into Creed's biceps, and her mind fluttered back to every time she'd been wrapped in his strong arms. Could she do this again? Was she ready to put her heart on the line?

CHAPTER NINETEEN

Kissing Kat felt right. It felt more than right. It felt like home.

Her lips held a hint of cherry. Her kiss was smooth as honey. She tasted just as he remembered. *Better.* Kissing her, touching her. It was as if he'd found the last piece of his puzzle. If he kept on, Creed would certainly scoop her up and press her into his bed. He'd explore much more than her lips. He'd spill more secrets. He'd tell her that he'd never stopped loving her.

But no matter how he felt about the woman who tightly clutched his arms, Kat had just broken up with her fiancé. She'd flat-out told Creed that she was confused. He wouldn't be her rebound. He couldn't handle it if Kat decided to go back to another man. To leave him again. No matter how hard it would be to stop kissing her, Creed couldn't do this until Kat knew what she wanted. Until she wanted to be with him.

As Kat slid her hands under his arms and around his back, Creed inched back from their kiss. Her eyes opened slowly, meeting his. They were hooded and full of need. Creed instantly wanted to crush his lips back to hers. His heart lurched when he told himself that he couldn't. A groan growled in his throat, purely from stifled desire.

All at once, alarm filled Kat's face. She let go of him.

"Your back," Kat gasped. "I'm so sorry. Does it hurt? Of course it does."

Creed's mind had to dig deep to understand what Kat was asking—*she* was the only thing he'd been thinking of.

"My back?"

Rodeo. Double-barrel kicked. Concussion. The day came back to him in pieces.

Now she looked really worried. "I think you better lie down." Kat looped her fingers around his wrist, and Creed nodded, using the excuse of his bruised back as a buffer for his heart.

"Yeah, maybe." He pushed a hand through his hair. His lungs were still pumping, his chest heaving. He hadn't thought of his back once as he'd kissed Kat.

"I'll get you some water." She stepped out of the bedroom, and Creed wanted a do-over. He should've never given up on her. Why had he let her run away? Why had he given another man the opportunity to win her heart? Now she didn't know what she wanted. And she *had* made another life—far away from Creed. She had a job, friends, a place of her own. Even if she didn't have a fiancé, she'd still go back to Chicago. After Jesse's wedding, Kat would leave Creed behind. Again.

By the time Kat came back into the bedroom, Creed was in bed and under the covers. He thanked her for the water, took a drink, and set the glass on the nightstand. Then he put his head back on the pillow, as if his insides weren't screaming at him to take hold of Kat again. As if he hadn't just shared a mind-blowing kiss with a woman he couldn't stop thinking about.

"Um, I'll come check on you in a few hours," Kat said awkwardly. "Try to sleep."

Creed didn't argue. He couldn't make sense of what he wanted to do or say. "Okay." At his one-word answer, Kat turned and left the bedroom.

Creed's sleep was fitful. His head had suffered more than just a concussion. When he did sleep, he dreamt of Kat. Of their time together. Of the past, present, and future. All of it upset him. Dreams of happy times were in the past. Dreams of hard times only reminded him of the mess he'd made. But there was one thing he found comfort in— waking up to Kat. She stayed with him all night, sleeping on the couch and rousing him every few hours. She'd rub his arm, bring him out of his dreams, and ask him a few questions.

"Do you know what day it is?" Kat whispered, rousing Creed again.

Creed opened his eyes. Kat's silhouette stood over him in the dark. She asked him the same questions every time she woke him, to make sure the concussion hadn't taken a bad turn.

"Thursday," he replied.

"Do you know what you did yesterday?"

That was a loaded question, but Creed knew Kat wasn't asking about their kiss. "Was at Sugar Springs Rodeo."

"Good." She stopped rubbing his arm. "Can you drink some more water?"

Creed propped himself up and took the glass from Kat. After he drank, he said, "You don't have to sleep on the couch. This bed is plenty big." Creed knew it would be tempting to have Kat sleep next to him, but he also didn't want her uncomfortable. He'd already tried giving up his bed for her. She wouldn't swap places with him.

She was rubbing the back of her neck like she had a kink in it. "No, I'm fine out there." She obviously wasn't.

"We can't both be hurting tomorrow," Creed urged. "I don't want to be responsible for you hobbling around at the groom's supper. I'll be doing enough of that for the both of us." He fluffed his pillow and rolled onto his back, feeling bruises seeping through muscle.

Kat stopped rubbing her neck. "Maybe I'll just lie down for a bit." She moved to the other side of the bed and crawled on top of the covers. Creed sighed, glad she wouldn't be scrunched up on his couch and surprised by how much he relaxed just having her near. Soon, he drifted off and slept deeper than he had all night. He slipped into more dreams of Kat—her bright eyes, mischievous smile, and contagious laugh. Subconsciously, he waited for Kat to reach over and rouse him, but it was Sasquatch's meows that woke him this time.

Creed groaned as his dream left and reality crawled in. *Why was Sasquatch meowing in the middle of the night?*

Creed started to roll over, to get out of bed and dump more food in Sasquatch's bowl before his meows woke Kat. But when Creed moved, he realized Kat was curled up next to him, under the covers. Creed's arm was hooked around her. She was spooned against him. Silky hair spilled over his arm, onto the pillow. A warm, toned leg was wrapped over his. Creed didn't want to move an inch. He wanted to stay like this forever. *If only it were that simple.*

Sasquatch meowed again, and Kat stirred. Creed vowed to get a bowl the size of a bucket so his cat never ran low on food again.

"Hi," Creed said, as Kat's arm stretched across his chest. Kat looked up at him and gave a little gasp. "Oh, hi."

"Do you know what day it is?" Creed tried to break the ice. "Do you know where you are?"

She gave a soft, nervous laugh. "I'm not sure what happened. I must've gotten cold."

Creed smiled and wondered if she could see his happiness through the dark. There was something about Kat that always made him feel better. Everything was sweeter when she was around, even when the rest of the world was harsh.

Creed figured Sasquatch could wait a little longer for his kibble, but an odd noise clinked in the kitchen, grabbing Creed's attention. He cocked his head. The noise sounded an awful lot like the door.

Kat stiffened. "What was that?"

Confusion quickly turned to alarm. Kat sat up and Creed threw the covers off them both. He stood, hoping he was just hearing things, but ready to square off with an intruder. He took two big strides out of the bedroom, and his stomach sank when he heard his name.

"Creed?" The female voice came from the kitchen.

Creed hit the light switch under the cabinets, illuminating the kitchen and living area. Zoey was standing by the sink, looking about as stunned as Creed was. She was wearing a coat and scarf. She had a brown paper bag in one arm and a tall thermos in the other.

"I—" Zoey stammered. "I heard you had a bad wreck at the rodeo. Just got off my shift. Brought you chicken fingers and fries. And hot chocolate. I thought—"

Zoey's eyes shifted behind Creed, and he knew why she'd stopped talking. Kat had scrambled off the bed with him.

"Zoey," Creed started, trying to figure out what he was supposed to say. He'd always been up-front with Zoey about their status. She wasn't his girlfriend. But did he care about her? Yes. And he hated to see the look that now crossed her face. It was like he'd just ripped her heart out with his bare hands. "This isn't—" He couldn't put his thoughts into truthful words that wouldn't cause her more pain.

Kat came up behind him and finished his sentence. "This isn't what it looks like." She straightened the sweater she'd been sleeping in. The one that had been cuddled up to his skin.

"It looks like you two were sleeping together," Zoey said, frozen to her spot near the sink.

"No." Kat repeated the word a few times. Creed's insides twisted each time she said it. "I was with Creed at the rodeo. He did have a bad wreck. A concussion. I stayed with him to make sure he was okay."

Zoey looked at Kat. Then at Creed. "None of that is what I wanted to hear," Zoey said before setting the paper bag and thermos on the counter.

"Zoey, can we talk? Outside?" Creed asked, but Kat scooted by him.

"It's okay. I'll leave. Let you two talk." Kat grabbed her purse and jacket from the table. She headed for the door.

Before she slipped outside, she gave Creed a look he couldn't read.

Creed wanted to tell Kat not to go, but also knew he couldn't avoid the talk he was about to have with Zoey. Zoey needed to hear the truth. That he wasn't in a place where he could have any kind of relationship with her—casual or serious. Not when his heart was still tethered to Kat. No matter what happened with Kat, Creed knew he had to be in a different place before he could give his heart away. To anyone.

CHAPTER TWENTY

Kat woke to Louise licking her forehead. When she opened her eyes, both dogs were on the bed, staring at her. They squirmed happily like she'd just arrived home from a long trip.

"Good morning," Kat mumbled and scooped both dogs to her chest. After giving them kisses, Kat wiped the sleep from her eyes and peered around her brothers' old bedroom. Sun streamed in through a crack in the curtains. She caught a whiff of bacon in the air. *What time is it?* Her laptop was on the bed, by her feet. Kat reached over and clicked the keyboard, bring the screen to life.

"Geez," Kat said, when it told her it was nine o'clock. She couldn't remember the last time she'd slept that late.

After leaving Creed's boat in the wee hours of the morning, Kat had snuck back into her parents' house. She'd crept upstairs and crawled into bed, but instead of sleeping, she had revised and finished her presentation. Work was the only thing that stopped her from obsessing over the day she'd had with Creed. The day that had been a rollercoaster of emotions—happiness, fear, elation, hurt, desire—and she was still trying to figure out if she should stay on the rollercoaster or jump off.

Was it normal to have a man stuck in your head for twenty years? Was there something wrong with her?

The accident in Sugar Springs confirmed how much Kat cared for Creed. It also confirmed how things had changed, at least for her. Kat had watched Creed compete at rodeos since they were teenagers. On bulls and broncs. Cheering him on used to thrill her, but watching him ride now brought about a different set of emotions. When Creed fell and the horse kicked him, fear lanced through Kat. She knew how easily life could slip away. Death wasn't picky. As Creed laid motionless on the arena dirt, Kat knew she couldn't lose him—which was a double-edged sword. Creed wasn't going to give up rodeo. Rodeo was part of him. If Kat let Creed consume her heart, she would be making a choice to be with someone who risked his life every time he got on a bronc. Could she be with Creed, knowing that?

Kat took another deep sigh and rolled out of bed. She needed a hot shower. And a gallon of coffee. Anything to clear her head.

Kat shuffled out of the bedroom and into the hall, headed toward the bathroom. Thelma and Louise joined her but bounded ahead, distracted by a wedge of sun that beamed across the hall floor. The dogs sniffed and followed the sunbeam—to Kat's old bedroom. The door was cracked open, and Thelma immediately wiggled through the space. Louise followed her sister.

Kat stared at the door, now suddenly awake. She hadn't been in her old bedroom—the one she'd shared with Sarah—since she'd moved to Chicago.

Tentatively, Kat stepped toward the door. She pushed it open.

Hinges creaked, and Kat laid eyes on a bedroom that looked more like a time capsule. Powder-pink walls. White lace curtains. Wooden bunkbeds blanketed in tie-dyed comforters and matching pillows. Posters of heartthrobs with bleach-tipped hair.

Kat stepped inside. Her feet sank into plush carpet. The same carpet she and Sarah had played dolls and board games on. In their teens, they'd laid on the floor, listening to music, doing homework, and sharing secrets. Thelma and Louise pranced by the matching dressers. Kat's dresser was on the right, topped with a stack of books and a framed picture of Diesel. On the left, Sarah's dresser was littered with scrunchies and makeup. Oval mirrors hung above both dressers. Kat looked at her reflection. She could picture Sarah there with her . . .

Curling her hair.

Laughing.

Dancing.

Telling a dramatic story.

Before she could stop herself, Kat went to her dresser and pulled open the top drawer. It was full of pictures and mementos, things Kat hadn't seen in over a decade.

She grasped an envelope of pictures—precious moments captured by a disposable camera—and fingered through them. They were from her senior year. There were pictures from rodeos, boating on the lake, barbeques, and campfires. Sarah's smile beamed through so many of the photos. Kat could hear her laugh. Each picture was full of joy, love, family, and friends. Kat saw the joy on her own face as well.

Setting down the pictures, she continued to pick through the drawer. There were tickets from the first concert Kat and Sarah ever went to—a boy band who danced better than they could sing. The first pair of leather spur straps she had won at Maple Bay Days, the local rodeo where she'd run barrels and poles along with her sisters. There were shells from the sandbar, rocks she'd saved from special walks along the lake, and dried corsages. Each memento took Kat back to a special memory, but her eyes widened when she spotted a handwritten note from Creed. The note was scrawled across a napkin in messy boy writing.

Meet me at the bar. ~ Creed.

"Bar" was secret kid-code for the sandbar in the middle of the lake, and Kat recalled the exact day she'd received this note. It was not long after they had officially started dating—the first time. Creed had left the napkin-note on her pillow, knowing she'd find it when she went to bed. When she did, Kat had snuck out of the house and took the rowboat to the sandbar. Creed was waiting for her with a crackling fire and a blanket. That night was the first time Creed had told her that he loved her. She'd eagerly said the words back, and they'd spent the night together, wrapped up in a blanket on the beach.

Kat touched the napkin, vividly remembering how full her heart had been that night. Could it ever be that full again?

As she stared at the napkin, Kat noticed a chain peeking out from behind it. She picked up the napkin and revealed two pieces of jewelry that tugged at her heart. Creed's note had been sitting on top of two *best friend* necklaces—one silver, the other gold. Each necklace held a charm which was half of a heart. When the two necklaces were placed together, the charms clicked together like puzzle pieces, making a full heart and completing the inscription of *best friends*.

The silver necklace was Kat's. The gold necklace was Sarah's.

Kat remembered the day she'd found the necklaces at a cheap jewelry store in the mall. They may not have cost more than a few weeks' allowance, but to Kat, they were priceless.

In one hand she held Creed's note. With the other, she picked up the necklaces.

As she stood there, the words Creed had said to her last night played in her head. *You can't heal by forgetting.*

She didn't want to forget.

"Kat?"

She turned to find her dad in the doorway. He gave her a sympathetic look, walked over, and pulled her into a hug.

Kat set her head on her dad's shoulder. Her ear pressed against his suspenders, and she closed her fingers around the necklaces. "I wish she was here."

"We all do, sweetie. We all miss her." Gene held her. "But we can't go backwards in time. The only thing we can do is forge on. We must all take steps forward, no matter how little or big those steps might be."

Kat nodded against her dad's shoulder. She was beginning to realize that. "Remembering Sarah is hard. But forgetting her is harder," she said. "I don't want to forget her. I want to remember her, always."

"We will," he said, tightening his hold around her shoulders. "We will remember Sarah, always. She will *always* be your sister. She will *always* be with you. And when it gets hard, you can lean on us. Lean on your family. You don't have to carry this load by yourself. That's not your burden to bear."

Kat let her dad's words settle in. Her family had been telling her a version of that since Sarah passed, but standing in her childhood bedroom, hugging her dad, holding a piece of Sarah, Kat was finally ready to hear it.

She lifted her head and gave her dad a tender smile. "I love you."

"I love you too."

Kat squeezed the necklaces in her hand. "Could you help me put these on?" She raised her hand, revealing the chains and charms.

"I'd love to," Gene said.

Kat turned to face the dressers and mirrors. She watched as her dad clasped each necklace around her neck. When the charms hung side by side, Kat felt like Sarah was with her.

It was the first time she had felt like her heart could be pieced back together—made whole—like the charms. Her heart wasn't meant to be broken.

Kat turned back to her dad. "Dad, I have something to tell you."

She raised her left hand and told her dad the truth about her engagement, releasing further guilt.

CHAPTER TWENTY-ONE

Kat's parents hosted the groom's dinner in the barn. There were at least fifty people, including the wedding party and extended family. Long tables ran down the middle of the barn aisle, draped with wheat-colored cloths and bundles of daisies. The horse stalls on either side were empty but doubled as décor. Strings of white lights hung across the stall fronts. Wreaths made of fall flowers and foliage added a pop of color to each stall door. The barn was full of laughter and excitement. Everyone wished Jesse and Hazel a lifetime of happiness, in between mouthfuls of barbeque.

Kat's cheeks hurt from smiling. It was good to be surrounded by family. To hear stories she'd heard a hundred times. See faces she didn't realize she'd missed so much.

After dinner, Kat helped to clear out serving bowls, crockpots, and foil pans to make room for apple pie. As she carried an empty crockpot to the house, she had to laugh.

There were at least six crockpots that her mom and aunts used to make dinner. Not a one of them was a *Genius Appliances* product. Kat was starting to wonder if her mom and aunties knew something that she didn't. The appliances they used were decades old, yet Kat couldn't deny the homecooked goodness that came out of them.

After cleaning up, Kat carried a few warm pies back to the barn and added them to the dessert table. As she did, Charlie ran up beside her.

"Can you get me a pie, Aunt Kitty Kat?" Charlie asked, out of breath.

"A whole pie?" Kat looked down at her adorable niece. She wore mini-sized Wranglers and a pink western shirt. Her shirt matched the bow in her hair and the boots on her feet. "How about a slice instead?"

Charlie pursed her lips like she wasn't sure about that. "A *big* slice, please?"

"You got it." Kat cut two slices of apple pie and put them on plates with forks. She handed one of the plates to Charlie. Charlie's eyes rounded like saucers, and she dug in.

"Daddy said I can ride my pony after this." Charlie licked her lips as she talked. "Can you ride with me and Grace?"

"I'll come watch you," Kat offered through a mouthful of apple, sugar, and spice.

"You can ride too. Daddy said Diesel is your horse, so you can ride him."

She slid Charlie a smile, not sure she was ready to get back in the saddle. "I would, but I haven't ridden Diesel in a long time. Actually, I haven't be on him since you were a baby."

Charlie stopped chewing and looked at Kat like she'd gone bonkers. "Why? I ride my pony all the time."

The answer to Charlie's question was a lot more than a five-year-old could handle. "Been busy," Kat replied. "But that's no excuse. I'd like to ride him again." Admitting that to herself forced Kat's heart to flutter, in a good way. "But he's probably a little rusty. Just like me. I don't think I should hop on him tonight."

Diesel was a sensitive horse and could be a little hotheaded. That combination made him a top-notch rodeo horse, but it also meant he needed regular riding and exercise to behave under saddle. Even at twenty-three years old, Diesel would be feisty if she brought him out of the pasture and just jumped on. And, being rusty herself, she wasn't ready for a feisty ride.

Charlie quirked an eyebrow at her just as Creed approached the dessert table and picked up a plate. "But Uncle Creed's been riding Diesel. If Creed can ride him, you can too. Right?" Charlie looked to Creed for confirmation.

Creed had a pie spatula in one hand and a plate in the other. He looked like he'd just been caught with a hand in the cookie jar.

"You've been riding Diesel?" Kat asked Creed.

Creed nodded and served himself a piece of pie. "Just for a couple of months." He grabbed a fork.

"How come?" Kat didn't mind. She just wasn't sure why he'd be riding her retired barrel horse when there was plenty of young stock at the Weston barn.

"I knew you'd be home for Jesse's wedding and thought you might like to ride while you were home. I just tuned him up a bit. He's plenty fit if you'd like to go for a ride."

Kat didn't know what to say. Creed had been exercising her horse? For months? On the off-chance that she *might* get back in the saddle when she was home for Jesse's wedding?

"That was," Kat fumbled for words, "really nice of you."

Creed shrugged like it was no big deal. Charlie patted him on the leg.

"Good job, Uncle Creed," she said. Her exuberance made Creed laugh. Charlie looked at Kat. "See, now you can ride with me."

"Sounds like I can." Kat said as she eyed Creed, thinking his gesture was sweeter than the forkful of apple pie she scooped into her mouth.

Kat, Charlie, and Grace went to retrieve their horses from the pasture. There was less than an hour left of sunlight, so they needed to get saddled quickly.

"You never met my horse?" Charlie asked Kat as they walked through the pasture, hand in hand. Grace held onto Charlie's other hand.

"No, I haven't." Kat knew Grace's horse, Chico. He was Jesse's retired roping horse, a been-there, done-that horse—the perfect horse to tote around kiddos. "What's her name?"

"Princess Sparkle Sugar Cookie," Charlie replied, a twinkle in her eye.

Kat chuckled. "That's adorable. Did you name her?"

"Uh huh." Charlie nodded, proudly. "There she is! Princess Sparkle Sugar Cookie, come here!"

Diesel, Chico, and Princess Sparkle Sugar Cookie were grazing together near a cluster of maple trees. The small palomino pony raised her head. In the evening light, her cream-colored mane and tail looked like frosting.

"I think that's the perfect name for her." Kat smiled, swinging Charlie's hand.

By the time Kat and the girls had haltered and walked their horses to the barn, Creed had a pile of brushes and tack sitting next to the hitching post.

"Since you can't take the horses into the barn, I thought it'd be easier if I brought everything out to you," Creed said.

"Thank you," Charlie and Grace both sang to Creed.

Kat gave him a smile. They hadn't talked since last night. Since the kiss. Since her abrupt departure from his boat.

Creed picked up a comb as Kat tied Diesel to the hitching post. "Mind if I help?"

"Not at all," she said.

"Here." Creed handed a stiff brush to Kat. When she took it, their fingers grazed and a wave of electricity blew through her, reminding her of how his hands had felt against her. Her cheeks heated, and she turned away to brush Diesel. "Where should we ride?" Kat asked the girls.

"Can we ride to the lake?" Grace asked, peeking over the top of Chico as she ran a brush over his back.

"Yeah!" Charlie chimed in. Creed was helping Charlie brush her pony, and Kat was instantly distracted by the sight of the tough cowboy combing Princess Sparkle Sugar Cookie's mane. She suppressed a smile.

Kat ran a brush over Diesel's long black-and-white striped mane. "I don't see why not."

When all three horses were brushed and tacked up, Frankie's boys showed up with their own rides. The three boys had run home to get their horses the instant they heard there was a chance of a trail ride. Frankie's youngest, Noah, rode a white pony that was even smaller and rounder than Charlie's pony. The two older boys rode double on a big, bay quarter horse. Frankie walked beside them.

"You sure you don't mind watching them all?" she asked Kat. "They can be a bit of a handful."

"No, it's fine," Kat said. "We're just going on a short ride, anyhow."

Frankie turned back to her sons. "You boys listen to Kat. Okay?"

Noah was trotting fast circles around the bigger horse. He was yelling "yeehaw" and circling his hand in the air like he had a pretend rope. Tommy and Wyatt were shooting at him with finger-pistols, squirming around in the saddle.

Kat suddenly wondered if she had bitten off a little more than she could chew.

Creed walked up beside Kat. "I can go with. Two adults might be better than one with this crew." He gave a sharp whistle and all three boys looked at Creed. "You guys got ants in your pants or what?"

The boys thought Creed's comment was hilarious and went into a fit of giggles. They also quit their shootout game.

"Yeah, that's probably not a bad idea," Frankie said, and patted both Kat and Creed on the arm. "Thanks, guys. I've got a glass of wine calling my name." She scooted off into the barn.

"Who will you ride?" Grace asked Creed, as she snapped the chin strap on her helmet.

"I'll just walk with you guys," Creed said. "I don't need a horse."

"Every cowboy needs a horse," Noah yelled like Creed's statement was offensive.

Kat helped Charlie get onto her pony. As Charlie plopped into the saddle, she said, "You can ride double with Kat. Just like Tommy and Wyatt." Charlie pointed to Frankie's boys.

Kat's eyes met Creed's. She wondered if her surprise had made it to her face.

"Nah, I can walk," Creed repeated.

Kat bridled Diesel. "You can ride with me." She gathered the reins and slid them over Diesel's neck. "I can't make you walk after you put in all the hard work on Diesel these past few months."

"It wasn't hard," Creed said.

"Well, it was thoughtful." Kat put a boot in the stirrup and threw a leg over Diesel. In the saddle, aboard her heart-horse, Kat instantly felt taller, prouder, lighter. She rubbed Diesel on his neck, forgetting her worries. Then she reached out to Creed. "Come on. Get up here."

CHAPTER TWENTY-TWO

Kat swayed in the saddle, inches in front of Creed. He was trying hard not to be distracted by the fruity, sweet scent of her shampoo or the way her hips sashayed with the rhythm of Diesel's walk.

"How does it feel?" Creed asked Kat. Diesel carried them both down the dirt path that circled the lake. Lapping waters and grassy shore bordered the right side of the path. Tall, colorful autumn trees edged the left. The kids rode in front of them.

"To ride?" she asked.

"Yeah, how's it feel to be back in the saddle?"

Her shoulders rose and fell with a breath. "Like heaven."

Exactly what he was hoping for. "I'm glad."

"Thank you for working Diesel. I don't think I would've had the gumption to get on him otherwise."

"My pleasure," Creed said.

A few months ago, when Creed had started exercising Diesel, he didn't think he'd end up on the horse *with* Kat. He just wanted to give her something that used to make her happy. He wanted to give her the opportunity to connect with her past, to find peace in the saddle. And, selfishly, he wanted to give her one thing he knew the other man in her life couldn't.

"I really appreciate it." Kat scratched Diesel's neck.

Creed was quiet, taking in the moment with Kat. He fiddled with the silver conchos on the back of the saddle, keeping his hands busy. He wanted to wrap his arms around Kat, hold her to his chest, but he wasn't sure he needed that. Did he want it? *Yes.* But needing and wanting were different beasts. He also didn't need his heart walloped when she left in a few days.

"Wow," Kat said. The ends of her honey-blonde hair brushed back and forth over her shoulders. "I remember being that little, riding with my brothers, sisters, and cousins. Such a special time."

The four horses carrying five kids poked along the path in front of Diesel. The kids joked and laughed as they rode.

"The next generation of cowboys and cowgirls." Creed gazed over Kat's shoulder at the kids he'd grown to love. In the short time they'd been on this earth, they'd each grabbed a piece of his heart. "Do you think you'll have kids of your own?" Creed nearly smacked his own forehead as the question left his tongue. Kat had just told him she'd broken off her engagement. Probably not the best time to bring up children.

She surprised him with a quick response. "I think so."

Creed rested his hands on his thighs, knowing Kat had changed her mind about having children over the years. When they were young, she'd wanted to get married, have a family. After college, she'd told him she didn't know, that she'd rather focus on her career. He wondered what had changed her mind.

"I think you'd be a great mom," he said. Kat poured her heart and soul into loving animals, always had. She had a strong maternal instinct and had grown up with amazing examples of what a parent should be. Joyce and Gene were the parents Creed always wished he'd had.

"Thanks." Kat paused before turning her head so he could see her profile. She tucked a lock of hair behind her ear. "And you? Could you see yourself having kids?"

"Me?" It wasn't that Creed didn't want kids. He just wasn't sure he was capable of being a dad.

Unlike Kat, Creed had grown up with messed-up and destructive parents. He'd inherited a weak spot for alcohol and knew there was always a chance he'd fall off the wagon. He'd do anything to keep that from happening, especially because he'd been part of the addiction rollercoaster his dad rode. But Creed knew it was always a possibility that he could succumb to his own demons. His urge to drink had never gone away. It sat inside him, and one bad decision could ignite it. If Creed stayed single, his bad decisions could only hurt himself. If he was married and had a family, falling back into the dark hole of drinking could ruin other peoples' lives. Those he cared about. He couldn't chance that. He'd witnessed the disaster his parents had painted, and he didn't want to paint one of his own.

"I've never really pictured myself with kids, but I love being an uncle to these rascals." He tried to make light of his response. Had he thought about having a family with Kat at one point? Yes. Did he think it was a good idea? No.

"You haven't thought about it with Zoey?" Kat asked. Her casual tone caught him off guard.

Have kids with Zoey? That question was so far off base that it took him a few beats to respond. Last night, he'd nearly lost himself in Kat. Had she not felt that too? Was last night just a lapse in judgement for her? Did she not hear him when he'd said that he and Zoey weren't together?

"Like I said, Zoey and I aren't together." Creed had made that clear to Zoey last night, after Kat left. He should've done it months ago.

"Oh," Kat replied, and Creed couldn't read her tone. Annoyed? Disappointed?

Instead of asking another question, Kat called to the kids. "Come on, guys. Let's turn around and head back home before it gets dark." The sun was starting to slip over the treetops.

As Kat reversed Diesel, Creed wanted to continue their conversation. He wanted to tell Kat that he'd ended things with Zoey. But the kids closed in quickly. Charlie and Noah rode their ponies up alongside Diesel, and the adult conversation came to an end. The rest of the ride was spent listening to the kids tell the story about the time Tommy fell into the manure spreader. It seemed appropriate. Creed felt like he'd just tripped into a mess himself.

When they got back to the barn, the last of family and friends were dispersing. Frankie walked her boys back to her place, a few houses over. Creed and Kat helped Charlie and Grace untack. After the horses were brushed and put back in the pasture, the girls ran off to the house. There were still a few family members congregated in the kitchen. Creed could see them chatting with Jesse and Hazel through the windows.

Kat grabbed an armful of brushes and bridles and disappeared into the barn. Creed picked up two saddles, one under each arm, and headed down the barn aisle behind her. When he stepped inside the tack room, Kat was hanging bridles on the wall rack.

"I'll get the other saddle," she said without looking at him. "Thanks for helping."

Creed heaved a saddle onto one of the saddle racks. "It's fine. I'll get it." He didn't like how she'd gone from warm to icy. After he put the second saddle away, he said, "Kat, do you have something you want to say to me?"

She looked at him over her shoulder, and he knew that face. It was the "I'd rather make you guess" face. He didn't like to guess.

"Spit it out," he said, knowing that would get a reaction out of her. He wasn't sure if it would be good or bad.

She turned toward him, shoulders squared. *That was not a good sign.*

"Why don't you want to be with Zoey?"

Creed reeled back. "I don't understand why you keep bringing her up? Are you upset because she showed up last night?"

"No." Kat paused and leaned against a cabinet.

He needed her to get to the point. "Kat, just tell me what the problem is." He wanted to fix it.

"I just," she started and frowned. "I don't understand why you don't want to settle down. Zoey seems like a nice person. She came to check on you in the middle of the night. She brought food and hot chocolate. She obviously cares about you. Why *wouldn't* you want to be with her?"

Creed's brows pinched together. *What?*

"I was never in a relationship with Zoey. I told her that from the start," he explained for what felt like the hundredth time. "We were casually dating. I wasn't—"

"So you just strung her along? Slept with her when it was convenient for you?"

Creed took in Kat's glare and crossed arms. He felt like she'd sucker-punched him. Mostly because she'd hit on the truth. He had done that. He'd kept Zoey around because he knew he could. She was a warm, kind body. A Band-Aid for his heart. She kept coming back to him, even when he pushed her away. On the opposite end of the spectrum, he'd *chased* the woman that stood before him. He'd begged and pleaded for Kat to give him another chance. She had shut him down. She'd forced him out of her life.

"I don't think you have a leg to stand on when it comes to what I do," he said. "You gave that up a long time ago. You're the one that left. Remember?"

Kat stiffened. Did she not realize how badly she'd crushed him when she left?

Her arms crossed tighter across her chest. "Are you ever going to change?"

"Change?"

"You can't commit to a relationship. You spend most of your time on the road and at rodeos. You're chasing a dream that could kill you."

Wow.

She might as well have shot out his knees. That was how Kat saw him? A roaming player chasing tail and lofty dreams? No wonder she ran from him.

Kat looked away for a few aching seconds. When she looked back, she looked broken, even though she had been the one to throw out the hurtful words. "I didn't mean that," she said.

"I think we're done here."

"Creed, that came out wrong." She started walking toward him.

He put a hand up, and she stopped. Creed turned and left Kat in the tack room.

It felt like he left his heart there as well.

CHAPTER TWENTY-THREE

The next day, Kat joined Hazel and her wedding party in the carriage house. They spent the morning primping in the second story, which was an old hayloft that had been converted into a beautiful apartment. When Hazel first moved to Maple Bay, she and Grace had lived in the apartment. Now that Jesse and Hazel lived together, Hazel mostly used the space to cook and bake for *The Carriage House Bed and Breakfast*. There was an open kitchen with white, farmhouse chic cabinets and stainless-steel appliances. Big picture windows lined the wall that looked out onto Maple Leaf Lake. Sunshine poured through the glass, warming the dark hues of the kitchen table, which held an array of curling irons, makeup, brushes, and sprays. Half-empty mimosas were also scattered throughout. A couple ladies from the local salon had done wonders with the wedding party's hair and makeup. Now, with less than an hour to the ceremony, Kat, Anne, Frankie, and Myra had changed into their bridesmaid dresses. The bride was next.

Joyce joined Hazel's adopted mother, Sandy, in the bedroom at the back of the apartment to help Hazel into her wedding gown. As they did, Kat sipped her mimosa. She wandered over to the wide windows and looked out at the picturesque fall day that would commence Hazel and Jesse's marriage. Rows of white chairs were lined up near the lake. In front of the chairs, there was a trellis covered in roses where they would exchange vows. Round tables draped in white linens bordered the carriage house, where dinner and dancing would take place tonight. And even though there was a pit in her stomach, Kat smiled. Regardless of her own state of mind, today was a happy day. She was thrilled for her brother.

Myra joined her at the window. Her ebony hair was rolled into a French twist accentuated by three white daisies. She took a long pull of her mimosa. "Well, you two are a sorry sight." She stared out the window with Kat. "What happened?"

Kat followed her cousin's gaze and found Creed. He was dressed in his slate-gray suit, standing on the deck off the backside of Jesse and Hazel's house. He gazed out over the lake like he was contemplating time. Even from a distance, he was unmistakably handsome. And infuriating.

Kat's lungs filled and released. "Nothing."

"Doesn't seem like nothing." Myra gave Kat a look like she wasn't fooled.

Disappointment rose in Kat's chest like heartburn. "I don't know why I keep coming back to him, Myra. I must be a glutton for punishment. I always expect things to be different, but it's like I'm running in a hamster wheel and always end up in the same spot. Except this time I feel like I tripped and fell on my head."

"Clarify, please," Myra said. "What were you expecting to be different?"

To have her own happily ever after. To get a kiss that didn't end in goodbye. To have the possibility of being with Creed forever.

"I never stopped thinking of him. Of Creed." Kat rolled her wrist, cracking it. "Even when I was engaged." Kat paused, thinking how sad that sounded. "But I don't think he'll *ever* settle down, and I just need to get the idea of him out of my head."

Easier said than done.

"Hmmm," Myra purred before taking another drink from her champagne glass. That was the sound she made when she was trying to bite her tongue.

"What? Tell me," Kat said. "I need some Myra advice right about now."

"Can you handle my advice?"

Kat pursed her lips. She wasn't sure. "Give it to me." She needed someone to straighten her out.

"Honey, I don't know if I'm even qualified to give advice on love, but I do know that doors open when they're ready to open." Myra looked Kat straight in the eye. "Do you really think you and Creed were meant to be together back then?"

Kat stilled like Myra had hit a nerve. "What do you mean?"

"When you were first together, you were so young. I know you thought you wanted to marry him straight out of high school, but I honestly think it would've been a disaster if you two had stayed together. You needed to go off to college, not become his wife. And Creed had some wild oats to sow and some serious issues to work through." Myra set a hand on Kat's arm, like she wanted to make sure Kat stayed to hear the rest of her advice. "And when you two got together again, before Sarah's passing, Creed was just getting sober. And you were restless in this small town. You both still had life to live, experiences of your *own* to have."

Myra's words drifted through Kat and settled like sediment.

Kat swallowed. Her eyes slid back out the window to Creed. He'd been joined on the deck by her brothers and her father. They were all laughing, probably to an inside joke no one else could know. She honestly couldn't picture her life or her family without Creed. He'd stumbled into their family unwillingly, but God had led him to the Westons. Kat was sure of that. Creed was meant to be her family. But was he meant to be *with her*?

"Talk to him," Myra continued. Kat looked at her. "Maybe you weren't meant to be together back then, but that doesn't mean you can't be together now. Only the two of you can figure that out."

"I tried to talk to Creed last night. About us," Kat replied, remembering how she'd snapped at Creed—simply because she was mad at herself for falling back into love with him. Being with Creed this past week had reminded her of all the things she loved about him. But could love ever be enough? Could love overcome their obstacles? Could Creed commit to her? Would he want to raise a family someday? Or would he blaze his own trail forever? "But I said all the wrong things."

Myra nodded. "So try again. Talk to him. Try different words this time."

Kat's lips turned up at her cousin's frank advice. She set her hand on top of Myra's. Then she hugged her. "I will."

"Good," Myra replied just before Frankie called the attention of everyone within earshot.

"Here comes the bride!" Frankie called.

Kat and Myra pulled out of their hug just in time to witness Hazel's entrance. Hazel walked out of the bedroom, beaming like the sun. Her white gown had an off-the-shoulder neckline and lace sleeves. It skated over her figure.

Her auburn hair was half up, with small white roses in her curls.

The whole room gasped and then circled the bride.

"Oh, Hazel. You look gorgeous," Kat said, tears springing to her eyes. "Jesse is going to die when he sees you."

"I hope not," Hazel jested. "I need him around for at least a hundred more years."

Kat smiled and blinked through blurry vision.

Joyce clutched Hazel's hands and kissed her soon-to-be daughter-in-law on the cheek. "We are so blessed to have you as part of this family. I know Rose is looking down, smiling her cheeky smile. And I thank my friend every day for placing you in our lives." Rose had been Hazel and Frankie's mother and Joyce's best friend. She was sorely missed.

Tears flowed. Kat reached out and grabbed Frankie's hand. She was crying as well.

Every day is a blessing. Kat should know that by now. *Don't take anyone for granted.*

She needed to say her piece to Creed, apologize for what she said. She hadn't meant to hurt him. And she needed to figure out if they were meant to be together or if they should finally go their separate ways, as friends.

"It makes me so happy that you're wearing Rose's brooch down the aisle," Joyce added, breaking through Kat's thoughts.

Hazel touched the golden rose that was pinned in her hair. She smiled. "Me too."

"You have something old, something new, and something blue," Anne said. "Do you have something borrowed?"

Hazel faltered for a beat. "Oh, I totally forgot. I was going to—"

Kat's fingers went to her own neck. "I have something for you." Kat reached up, unclasped the gold *best friend* necklace, and pulled it out from under the high, silky neckline of her bridesmaid dress. "It's Sarah's necklace. *Something borrowed.*" The room fell silent, like a prayer. "We could tie it to your bouquet." Kat wanted to offer something near and dear to her heart but didn't expect Hazel to walk down the aisle wearing a ten-dollar necklace.

Hazel stepped toward Kat. "Can I wear it? Please?"

Kat's eyes misted over again. She nodded before reaching up and clasping the chain around Hazel's neck. The necklace laid perfectly next to two strings of pearls. Then Kat hugged Hazel, knowing she was the perfect addition to their family.

"Welcome to the family, sister. We're so happy to have you. I know Sarah would approve."

CHAPTER TWENTY-FOUR

Creed stood just outside the carriage house, staring at the tall, open barn door. Evan stood in front of him. Frankie's husband, Garrett, was behind. Jesse had already walked down the aisle with Joyce and Gene. Music floated through the air, and the first of the bridesmaids appeared—Frankie stepped out of the carriage house. Evan approached her, offered his arm, and they started down the aisle to join Jesse at the trellis.

Creed was up next. His heart was beating awfully hard for an organ that had been crushed yesterday, but he didn't have to worry about the erratic beating for long. It came to an abrupt stop when Kat came into sight. Her long, emerald-green dress was tied at her neck and cinched at her waist. The skirt swished gracefully as she walked toward him. Her blonde hair was gathered in a loose bun at the nape of her neck. White daisies decorated it like a barrette. She clutched a bouquet of yellow roses.

When she got close to him, Kat bit her bottom lip and Creed almost forgot to offer up his arm. He could not take his eyes off her.

Kat smiled and reached for him. Creed jerked out of his stupor.

"You look like an angel." He couldn't keep the thought to himself, no matter how his heart hurt.

She placed a hand in the crook of his arm. "I don't deserve that."

"You always deserve that."

She clutched his elbow, looking timid. "I'm no angel, and I'm sorry for what I said last night. It honestly came out all wrong. Will you give me a chance to explain? Tonight?"

He nodded. There were things he wanted to say to her as well. And they certainly couldn't talk now. Creed smiled, and Kat returned his gesture. Then they walked, arm and arm, down the aisle. Family and friends watched them, all in their Sunday best, and Creed felt like he could breathe again. At the end of the aisle, Kat squeezed his arm before they separated and moved to opposite sides of the trellis.

As Creed passed Jesse, he gave him a solid pat on the shoulder. "Love you, man."

Jesse returned the sentiment, and Creed took his place at Jesse's side, next to Evan.

Garrett wasn't far behind. He accompanied both Anne and Myra down the aisle, completing the bridesmaids and groomsmen. Then the whole crowd cooed as Noah, the ringbearer, appeared in his miniature suit. Halfway down the aisle, he started running, not able to wait to get the pillow and ring to Jesse. Everyone laughed. Then they cooed again when Grace and Charlie started down the aisle. The girls held hands and wore matching emerald dresses. Charlie tossed rose petals from a small basket that Grace carried. They looked like little princesses. The sight forced a lump into Creed's throat. He swallowed and looked at Kat. She was crying, tears cascading over a brilliant smile.

When Hazel appeared in the carriage house doorway, the whole crowd stood, but Creed couldn't take his eyes off Kat. He wanted to wipe away those glistening tears. He wanted to dry her tears and make her laugh for the rest of his life. He couldn't imagine being with anyone but her. If she wouldn't have him, he knew no one else could.

Afternoon melted into evening, and soon everyone was seated at the round tables near the carriage house, enjoying dinner. As they ate, heartfelt speeches arose from the wedding party. Frankie's speech had everyone crying. Evan's speech had the crowd roaring with laughter. And when Hazel and Jesse announced that they were expecting a baby, there was a standing ovation. Creed whistled and hooted, overjoyed for his friends and their growing family.

After the cake cutting, dinner spilled into dancing. A local cover band played songs that packed the patio off the back of the carriage house. *Twist and Shout. YMCA. Sweet Caroline. Friends in Low Places.* Jesse and Hazel were busting out moves. Kids zipped around the patio and through the lawn. Kat's grandpa Vern was doing the boot scootin' boogie with anyone that wanted to dance. The entire wedding party was shimmying and shaking.

When an upbeat country song started, Kat took hold of Creed's arm. "You remember this?" she asked, her cheeks flushed from dancing.

The band was playing a song that was a regular tune at *The Silver Saddle*, especially on Two-Steppin' Tuesdays. Kat and Creed had danced to it many times.

Creed pulled her in close, wrapping one hand around her waist. He took her other hand with his free hand. "The better question is can you keep up?" His taunt pushed her into a surprised smile.

"Oh, I can keep up." She popped her eyebrows at him. Creed thought she was going to motivate him with her "I dare you" trick. He didn't wait for it. He walked toward Kat, following the beat, and led her into a two-step.

Quick, quick. Slow, slow. Quick, quick. Slow, slow. She matched his every move with a sway in her hips and a shuffle to her step. The crowd started clapping to the beat. Frankie and Garrett joined them. The bride and groom followed. Soon the patio was full of two-stepping couples.

Creed turned Kat to the right. Twisted her to the left. He sent her out into a twirl like a cowgirl ballerina, her emerald skirt spinning about her feet. She came back to him, an unmistakable sparkle in her eye. A laugh bubbled from her lips. Creed pulled her in close, sure the grin on his face couldn't get wider.

"I think we could do this in our sleep," he said.

Kat bit her lip, looking like she was having the time of her life. Creed wanted to make her feel that way, always.

Quick, quick. Slow, slow. Quick, quick. Slow, slow. Their feet matched his leaping heart.

"You're still the best two-stepper I've ever known," Kat said to him.

Creed pressed their intertwined hands to his chest and soaked in every step he had with her. "Same."

As the song neared the end, Creed snuck in one more spin. Then he dipped Kat. She crooked her leg in the air and scrunched her nose up in delight. He held her in the dip, even as the next song started.

"Again?" she whispered.

How could he say no? Creed winked at Kat and stood her upright. They danced to a few more songs, until Creed's legs started to resemble jelly.

At the end of a particularly fast song, Kat pressed her hand to his chest. "Do you want a water?" She was breathing hard and smiling.

He nodded and pulled a handkerchief from his pocket to wipe the sweat from his forehead. "That'd be great."

"Be right back. Don't you go anywhere. I've got plenty of dancing left in me. I've been saving up all my two-steps."

"Don't you go dancing in Chicago?" he asked.

"Not like this." Kat disappeared into the carriage house.

Creed was walking on a cloud. He took a minute to steady himself.

"You might wear out your soles tonight," Frankie said to him, as she and Garrett twirled by.

"I hope so," Creed admitted. He'd gladly wear out his boots if that meant he got to dance with Kat for the rest of the night.

Waiting for Kat to return, Creed chatted with Myra and Evan, but when his heart rate neared normal, Creed decided he'd waited long enough. He needed to find her. The band only had a few songs left, and he wanted his partner back.

Inside the carriage house, Creed scanned the crowd. He caught a glimpse of Kat's blonde bun near the fireplace. Starting toward her, he passed the cake table and bar. He wound around folks, making small talk as he passed. When he neared Kat, he saw that she was on the phone. He slowed his stride, not wanting to intrude, but also wondering who she was talking to. It was nearly midnight. All her family was here, at the wedding.

Kat's back was to him. He should've turned around, gone back outside to wait for her. But his feet stopped when he overheard her conversation.

"I'm so glad you called, Michael," she said.

Michael? Kat was talking to her ex-fiancé?

Creed's chest stilled. He wasn't sure if he wanted to step closer or back away.

"Yes, the wedding is beautiful. Thank you," she continued. "Gosh, that's such wonderful news."

The trill of her voice choked him. She was excited. Had she been waiting for Michael to call?

Kat bounced on her toes. "Yes, I'm coming back tomorrow night." She leaned against the stone fireplace and turned her head just enough so that Creed could see her profile. "Of course. I'll act surprised." Her eyes and smile were bright. *She was happy.* "Yep. I'll see you then."

As Kat said good night to Michael, Creed stepped back. Realization hit him in the chest like an arrow. Earlier— before they walked down the aisle together—Kat had asked Creed if they could talk. She'd said she wanted a chance to explain. *Explain what?*

That Michael was trying to win her back? That she was considering getting back together with him?

He shook his head but couldn't unsee Kat's happiness. Tomorrow she'd go back to the life she'd been living in Chicago, with the man that had proposed to her. She'd go back to the life she'd made *without* Creed.

Not wanting her to witness his deflating face, Creed turned and walked away.

CHAPTER TWENTY-FIVE

Kat had been surprised when her phone rang and Michael's name showed on the screen. She'd picked up, thinking there was an emergency of some kind, but relaxed when he started talking and eased her worries. He was out at a bar with friends and had a piece of information he couldn't keep to himself.

"I just had to call and tell you," Michael said, sounding a little tipsy. "I know I'm not supposed to, but I just couldn't wait." Being the human resources manager for *Genius Appliances*, Michael was the first to know when jobs were filled and positions were accepted. And as of yesterday, the board had decided that Kat would be offered the promotion to national sales manager.

"Gosh, that's wonderful news," she said into the phone. It was the position she'd been working towards since she started at *Genius Appliances*.

"You're back home tomorrow?" Michael asked.

"Yes, I'm coming back tomorrow night."

"Perfect. The board wants to offer you the position on Monday. I'll be in the meeting, so act like it's a surprise. Okay?"

"Of course. I'll act surprised." She smiled.

"Great. I'll see you tomorrow."

"Yep. I'll see you then."

"Congratulations, Kat. You deserve it."

Kat ended the call by thanking him. Then she stared at the crackling fire in the fireplace. She was happy to hear the news about her promotion, but as soon as she got off the phone, her first thought was to hurry up and get back to the dance floor. With Creed. With her friends and family. Work could wait. Getting back to reality could hold off for another day.

When she turned, she caught Creed exiting the carriage house. She grabbed two bottled waters from the bar and hurried out onto the patio, ready for another dance, wanting to be back in Creed's arms.

But when she stepped out onto the patio, she didn't see him. The band was playing *Sweet Caroline* for the second time tonight. Everyone swayed and sang along.

Kat approached Myra. "Have you seen Creed?"

Myra stopped her yell-singing. "He was just here." She spun on her tiptoes and then pointed toward the lake. "There he is."

Kat headed off in Creed's direction, away from the music and bustle. Creed was just past the dock, walking toward Jesse and Hazel's house. Maybe this would be a good time to talk to him? To explain why she'd gotten upset yesterday. "Creed," she called, now jogging across the lawn. "Can we talk now?"

He looked over his shoulder at her. "I don't think so."

The smile fell from her lips. "What?" She caught up to him and put a hand on his arm. "Hey, wait. Stop. What's going on?"

He turned to her. His entire demeanor had changed.

"What happened?" Kat asked, anxiety gathering in her gut. Something was wrong. Very wrong. "Are you okay?"

"I heard you on the phone with Michael." Creed paused. His eyes held a sadness she hadn't seen in a long time. "Are you getting back together with him?"

"What?" Kat blinked like Creed was a pair of headlights, staring her down. "No, I'm not getting back with—"

"It's okay if you are." His words were soft. Kat was surprised by how easily they cut her.

For a few long breaths, she couldn't reply. Why would he say that?

"Do you want me to get back together with him?" she asked, her brows furrowed in confusion.

Creed looked to the sky, seeming to search for an answer in the heavens. "I want you to be happy." When he looked back at her, his jaw squared. "You deserve so much more than I can give you. My life is on the road. At rodeos. Yours is in Chicago. You're leaving tomorrow. We live different lives. We can't continue down this path."

The path where she was falling for him? And he was running away?

"What are you saying?" Kat felt like he'd spun her into a dance move but she'd lost her footing and ended up on the floor.

"I wish you the best, Kat. I need you to know that. You deserve the best." Creed close his eyes for a beat. "And that's not with me." Then he turned and walked away.

A sharp pain jolted through Kat's chest. She meant to retort, to explain the phone call, to yell at Creed and make him come back and talk to her. But his words had sliced her to her core. In a few short sentences, he'd confirmed what she'd feared. Rodeo would always be his first love. And he was not ready to commit to a relationship . . . not with her.

So instead of running after him, she stood there—silent and bleeding—as Creed walked away.

CHAPTER TWENTY-SIX

The next morning, Joyce and Gene hosted a brunch in honor of the newlyweds. The kitchen island was full of breakfast casseroles, sausage links, muffins, and orange juice. Two coffee makers ran nonstop.

Halfway through the brunch, Kat busied herself with the dirty dishes. She filled one side of the sink with soapy, hot water and scrubbed at plates and silverware. She was trying to distract herself from thinking of Creed. She'd hoped to see him one last time before she left, but he hadn't shown his face at brunch.

"Honey, we can do those later," Joyce said as she filled her coffee mug.

Kat smiled at her mom. "You've done enough work. Go. Enjoy. I've got this."

"I'll help her." Myra grabbed a dish towel and joined Kat at the sink. She took a wet plate and wiped it dry. That seemed to satisfy Joyce.

"Thank you, girls." Joyce headed back into the living room to chat with her guests.

Myra opened a cabinet and set the plate inside. "So, spill it."

Kat scrubbed extra hard on a serving spoon. When she thought she might rub off the silver, she said, "Creed and I didn't leave on such good terms last night."

"I figured." Myra pried the serving spoon from Kat's fingers. "What happened?"

"Michael called me, and Creed overheard my conversation with him."

Myra quirked an eyebrow. "Michael called you? Last night?"

"Yeah, but it wasn't what you're thinking." Kat fished through the soapy water to grab another plate. "He called to tell me I got the promotion I've been wanting. That I'm going to be offered the position on Monday."

Myra slid the serving spoon into a drawer. "And that's good, right?"

"Yeah," Kat said, forcing optimism into her voice. It *was* good. She'd been working hard for years to land that position. It was exactly what she wanted. She shouldn't be feeling all doom and gloom. "I think it just hasn't set in yet. I'm sure it will hit me once I get back to Chicago."

"Well, congratulations. I'm happy for you."

"Thanks." Kat washed off the plate she'd just scrubbed. She handed it to Myra. "I tried to explain to Creed what my phone conversation was about, but he didn't want to hear it. It was like he'd already made up his mind that I was going to get back together with Michael."

"But you're not, right?"

"No, I'm not." Kat took a breath. "But maybe he was right to be upset? I lied to him. Told him I was engaged when I wasn't." She'd lied because she was terrified of another heartbreak. But she had never truly explained that to Creed. "No wonder he made assumptions."

"Don't beat yourself up. You weren't ready to talk about it. You told everyone eventually, right?" Myra asked. "Creed should've given you a chance to explain."

Kat nodded, guilt riddling her. "I was hoping to talk with him today. I don't want to leave on such bad terms. I even went to his boat last night, but he wasn't there." Kat squeezed out the sponge. She wanted to clear the air with Creed, let him know how much he meant to her. If nothing else, he needed to hear that.

Myra was silent. Plates clinked as she put them away.

"Why are you being weird?" Kat asked.

Myra twisted her lips. "Creed left for a rodeo in North Dakota."

A handful of silverware slipped out of Kat's hand and back into the sudsy water. "What? How do you know?"

"He texted me last night. I saw it when I got home. Said he'd be gone all week and asked if I could check on his cat."

Kat steadied herself against the sink. She pulled the plug and let the dirty water slug down the drain, much like her hopes. She finished washing the last of the silverware and handed it to Myra.

"Kat, are you okay?"

Kat dried her hands. "I'm fine." She was nowhere near fine. On top of pushing her away, Creed was blatantly ignoring his own safety. He was headed to another rodeo where one slipup could cause him major harm. He wasn't supposed to get on another bronc for at least a month. Creed did not *need* to take that risk. He could end up in a wheelchair, with brain damage, or six feet under the ground. Any result other than a safe ride would break her. Because after this week, Kat knew she loved him.

Even if he didn't love her back.

Leaving Maple Bay was hard. By the time she got to the airport, Kat felt like a piece of her was missing. That emptiness stayed with her all the way to Chicago where Kat made a conscious effort to pack her week with work and activity. When she wasn't in front of her computer or in a boardroom, Kat ran her anxieties out on a treadmill or along Lake Michigan. But she couldn't run from her true feelings—that the path she was on might only be a detour. That her destination didn't involve city lights or a demanding corporate position. That true happiness was waiting for her at home . . . in Maple Bay. With her family. And possibly with Creed.

Now, after nearly a full week working in her dream job, Kat sat in her new corner office and stared at her desk. A beautiful view of the Chicago skyline surrounded her, but she'd been looking at excel sheets so long that her eyes had nearly crossed. She hadn't even noticed when the sun set. It was eight o'clock on a Thursday night, and Kat was still at work, surrounded by an empty office.

Sitting back in her plush desk chair, Kat let a whoosh release from her lungs. Her shoulders were tight. Her rear was sore from sitting. Her head hurt.

After accepting the position on Monday, Kat dove into her new responsibilities with full force. And she now sympathized with Wendy—somewhat, at least. *Genius Appliances* put a lot of pressure on their sales team, and most of that was upheld by the national sales manager. On Monday, Kat received her marching orders for the next quarter, and all her goals revolved around getting sales on the newest products, which included the over-the-top crockpot that looked like a spaceship . . . the one her mom had politely said she hated. It didn't seem like Kat's new boss cared who she sold the product to or how she got the sales. The company simply wanted to see dollars flow in. That was the only thing that mattered. And the company's goals went against Kat's personal standards. She was motivated to make lasting relationships with clients, not to make a quick sale simply to hit quarterly goals and appease stockholders.

"Ugh." Kat sighed and closed her laptop. She glanced at her phone only to be disappointed again. Creed *still* hadn't called or texted her.

As soon as she got back to Chicago, Kat had called him. His phone was off, and her call went straight to voicemail, but she'd left him a message, explaining her conversation with Michael the night of the wedding. She also told Creed how much he'd helped her this past week, that he'd been the reason she'd been able to see the light, been able to start forgiving herself for past mistakes. Then she asked him not to get on a bronc, at least not until he'd healed. If he wouldn't do that for himself, she asked him to do it on behalf of all the people in his life who loved him.

That had been five days ago and he still hadn't called her back.

Standing up, Kat grabbed her coat. She couldn't work anymore tonight. As she left the office, passing empty cubicles, she called Lei. Her friend picked up on the first ring.

"Are you done yet?" Lei asked. Mariachi music played in the background. "I've got our booth, and I ordered you a mango margarita."

Kat smiled, despite her stress. "I'll be there in ten minutes."

After two mango margaritas, Kat spilled everything to Lei. How she'd worn her ring, faking her engagement. How that hadn't stopped her feelings for Creed. How he made her heart pound even when she didn't want it to. The car crash into the muddy field. The dive into the lake to save Thelma. The rodeo and Creed's accident. The kiss on his boat. The dancing. The overheard phone call. And their last conversation.

On the opposite side of the booth, Lei's mouth hung open. Her dark eyes blinked at Kat through red-framed glasses. "Oh my flipping goodness," Lei said. "You've been living in a rom-com for the past week, and it sounds *awesome*. How do I sign up for that? Can I have a cute cowboy too? Why did you leave?"

Kat stuffed a tortilla chip in her mouth. "It's not *that* awesome."

"It *sounds* awesome. Don't forget I got an eyeful of that cowboy on our video conference call. If someone looked at me the way I saw him look at you, I wouldn't have come back to Chicago. I'd have shacked right on up with that man. I don't care if he lives on a boat. Heck, he could live in a tent for all I care." Lei took a slurp of her strawberry margarita and licked salt off her lips. "So why *are* you back here?"

Kat gave her friend a glare. "Because I work here. Plus, I missed you."

"Well, of course you missed me." Lei shrugged her shoulders and gave Kat a cute smile. "I missed you too, but please don't let me be the reason you miss out on the potential love of your life. And for goodness' sakes, *please* don't let the money-grubbing conglomeration that is *Genius Appliances* be the reason you miss out on your happily ever after."

Kat sat there, pondering her friend's words. Kat had worked so hard to get where she was, but would this job make her happy? Would working endless hours for a company that didn't care about her or their clients fill her heart? Could she continue living a plane ride and a four-hour drive from her family?

"I can't just up and quit my job," Kat said, the common-sense side of her brain speaking up.

"I'm not telling you to quit. Not right now anyhow," Lei replied. "Use some more vacation days and go back home. Figure it out. Don't leave any stone unturned until you know for sure what you want."

Lei was onto something with the "figure it out" part. Kat would always wonder "what if" unless she fully laid out her feelings for Creed. He needed to hear what she had to say. Even if he wasn't ready for it. And if she told him that she loved him and he still walked away, then she would close that door. For good.

But maybe he still loved her too? Maybe there was a way to make it work between the two of them? She needed to know. Even if that meant opening her heart . . . and risking it being broken, again.

Kat took a big slurp of her margarita. "Lei, you're the only *genius* I need in my life."

"Duh," Lei replied with a smirk.

CHAPTER TWENTY-SEVEN

When Creed took off in the middle of the night, he'd purposely set his cell phone on his kitchen counter and left it there. He knew Myra would take good care of Sasquatch. No one else would need to reach him while he was gone. But most importantly, he didn't want to have a weak moment and call Kat. He needed space and time to think. He figured a rodeo or two would let him do that.

Except that instead of gaining a clear head, every second of silence was filled with thoughts of Kat. Every moment they'd shared in the past week was branded into his brain. It ran on a never-ending loop. He couldn't stop thinking of her.

Was she safe? Was she sleeping? Was she happy? Was she thinking of him as well? Had she run back to Michael?

The last question was like a knife to his chest. The blade had gotten stuck there, and Creed was trying everything possible to jerk it out. He'd driven to the middle of North Dakota for a rodeo on Sunday, the day after Jesse's wedding. It was cold, windy, and wet, but Creed held tight to a whipping bronc, only to be disappointed when his feet slopped into the arena mud at the end of a winning ride. Instead of elation, the first thing Creed thought of was Kat. As his boots pushed through mud, he pictured that stupid, tiny rental car stuck in the muddy field outside of Maple Bay.

After the rodeo on Sunday, Creed stayed at a friend's cattle ranch just outside of Bismarck. He helped with projects around the ranch—vaccinating calves and mending fence. It was good to work with his hands, to have something to focus on, to feel productive. Regardless, the painful blade was still stuck in his heart. When Friday rolled around, Creed drove to Fargo, craving another rodeo. It would be his last chance to rodeo close to home until spring, but Creed had already planned a road trip down south to continue riding over the winter.

As he pulled into the fairgrounds and added his truck to the familiar circle of trucks and trailers, Creed deflated like balloon, letting his breath pour out. He needed this. *The rodeo. The people.*

The regulars were already here. A campfire crackled in the center of the gathered trailers. Ellie and Destin stood by the fire, sipping from thermoses. They waved a greeting at him. Creed got out of his truck and joined them.

"So good to see you," Ellie said brightly, giving Creed a big hug.

"Hey, buddy," Destin hugged Creed as well. "We weren't sure we'd see you after what happened last week. How you doing?"

Both Ellie and Destin looked concerned. Creed brushed it off.

"Oh, I'm fine. Doing great," he said, which couldn't be further from the truth. But maybe if he said it enough times, he'd start to believe it.

"You riding tonight?" Destin asked like he hoped Creed would say no.

"Yeah," Creed zipped up his jacket, warding off the wind. When Ellie gave him another worried look, Creed changed the subject. "Which horses did you guys bring for the weekend?"

Ellie and Destin listed off their herd. Ellie had brought a young horse that had never been in a stadium arena. She was nervous for how he'd handle it. Destin had brought his trusty roping horse, and they'd trailered a few horses for friends as well.

Once Creed got Ellie and Destin talking horses, their attention waned off his questionable decision to get on a bronc after suffering a concussion. He didn't think their prodding was over, but he was here to ride. Nothing was going to stop him.

As a few more regulars joined them at the campfire, Creed got lost in everyone's stories and laughter. He was quiet, soaking in the camaraderie and thankful for the distraction. When it was time for him to grab his duffle bag and head to the chutes, Quinn the rodeo clown came jogging toward the fire with two funnel cakes.

"Hey, Creed!" Quinn yelled over the fire. He was dressed in his rodeo clown gear—overalls, a checkered shirt, and a floppy cowboy hat. His face was painted white and red, but it didn't conceal his huge smile. "Did you see the baby yet?"

Creed instantly remembered how pregnant Hannah had looked at the Sugar Springs rodeo. "What? When?"

"The last night of the Sugar Springs rodeo." Quinn craned his head toward the trailer. "Come on, he's awake now."

Creed met Quinn at the trailer and opened the door for his friend, whose hands were full. Quinn stepped inside, funnel cakes first.

"Hannah? Creed's here, and he wants to see the baby."

Creed stepped into the trailer and got attacked by two little rugrats. "Hey, you guys." He scooped the two young boys into his arms. Hannah and Quinn's twin daughters were sitting at the table, coloring. They waved. Hannah sat across from them, a tiny, swaddled baby in her arms. The smile on her face shone like a new penny.

"This is Joseph," Hannah said to Creed as she rocked the baby.

Quinn set the two funnel cakes on the table. "Another boy," Quinn said, looking at Creed like he'd won the lottery. Creed thought that he had.

"Wow, congratulations, you guys." Creed looked at them both in amazement. He didn't want to be jealous, but deep down, he was. He wanted this. He wanted a wife and family to share his life with. "He's absolutely beautiful. Has your eyes." Creed nodded at Hannah. "And your nose." He smiled at Quinn.

"I think so, too," Quinn replied.

After Creed mussed with the kids and repeated his congratulations, he headed out of the trailer and toward the chutes, feeling emptier than ever. It was as though his insides had evaporated. How had he gotten to this point? What was he doing with his life?

Jogging up the stairs to the platform behind the chutes, familiar faces waved and slapped him on the back, but all Creed wanted to do was get on a bronc. He started his normal routine—dressing in chaps, putting on his vest, lacing up his glove. It was then that he wished he had his phone. If he could stick in earphones and turn on his playlist, a few electric guitars would cut through his muddled thoughts. Creed stretched and restlessly jogged in place, but when he walked toward his designated chute, music struck him in a different way. Over the arena loudspeakers, a familiar song played. Creed recognized it in the first few cords. It was the song that most reminded him of Kat—the song they'd sung their lungs out to on the way to Sugar Springs.

Summer Love, Forever on my Mind.

He stopped, frozen in place, as the lyrics rang out over the arena and hit him in the chest.

"Hey, Creed. You're next," one of the rodeo staff called from his place on the chute panel. When Creed didn't answer, the man tipped his cowboy hat up, taking a good look at Creed. "You ready?"

Creed glanced from the cowboy's expectant face to the glare of the bronc. The black horse shifted side to side, ramming against the gate. Usually, that would amp Creed up, get his adrenaline pumping. But instead of excitement, Creed pictured Kat's face. In particular, he remembered her stark fear as he was carried into the medical tent on a stretcher.

The knife twisted in his heart.

He thought of Kat's laugh, her touch, the way she made him feel. How she'd been his cheerleader through so many ups and downs. She was the person he knew he wanted to be with.

The blade slid out, leaving a hole he desperately needed to fill.

"Come on, Creed. You're up," the cowboy said, getting impatient.

Creed shook his head. This wasn't where he belonged. He didn't want this high. Not anymore. He had somewhere else to be.

Creed drove faster than he should've to Maple Bay, but he managed to soar down the highway on luck, steering clear of speeding tickets and deer. By the time he parked on the dead-end road that faced his boat, it was after ten o'clock. The sky was inky black, but he would call Kat the second he got to his phone. He needed to tell her how he felt. He could book a flight and get on a plane tomorrow. Heck, if he started now, he could drive to Chicago and be there by morning. He would lay it all out on the line, make sure she knew everything. He wanted to be with her, no matter what it took. He would fight for her. He was the one she should be with, not Michael.

Jogging onto the dock and into his boat, Creed clicked on the lamp. Sasquatch was curled up on the couch. He meowed and stood to stretch.

"Hey, buddy." Creed gave him a quick scratch on his orange head and then went straight to the kitchen counter—where he'd stupidly abandoned his phone. Nerves surfaced as he neared, anticipating the call he was about to make, but his eyes widened when he saw what lay next to his phone.

On the counter, there was a white napkin. A message was scrawled across it in blue ink.

Meet me at the bar. Love, Kat.

CHAPTER TWENTY-EIGHT

Kat sat on a blanket draped over the sand, looking out over Maple Leaf Lake and into the dark night. From her spot on the sandbar, she could faintly see the glowing streetlights of Main Street. A sky full of twinkling stars shown down on her. When her phone rang, Kat grabbed it like it might run away. She sighed when the screen said *Mom* instead of *Creed*.

Kat picked up the call. "Hey, Mom. I'm okay. I promise. You and Dad can go to bed. I'll probably stay out here for another hour or so. I'll wake you when I get back to the house." Kat didn't want her parents to worry. She'd been camped out on the island for hours—four hours, to be exact—hoping Creed would respond to her call or her note. She hoped he'd come find her.

So far, no luck.

This afternoon, she'd packed her dad's fishing boat with a big blanket, a picnic basket of treats, and a few armfuls of firewood. Now, the treats were eaten and she'd just thrown the last piece of wood on the dying fire. Kat had come back to Maple Bay for Creed, to talk with him face to face. Myra had said he was supposed to be home tonight—after his ride in Fargo.

"Oh, honey," Joyce responded over the phone. "You know I won't be able to sleep until you come home."

Kat bit her lip, wondering if she should head back. It was after ten o'clock and pitch black. If Creed wasn't home yet, he might've stayed in Fargo for the night.

"I know, Mom. I'll head home soon. Just got to put the fire out."

"Don't leave yet," Joyce replied. "Not on my account. I can sleep when I'm dead. I called to tell you Creed is back in Maple Bay."

Kat's stomach flipped. "What? How do you know?" When Kat had arrived at her parents' house earlier in the day, she'd told them what she planned to do. They were beyond supportive, telling her she needed to follow her heart.

"Judy called. She was out in her garden trying to shoo away this nasty little squirrel that keeps eating from her bird feeder," Joyce said. Kat pictured Aunt Judy in a nightie, swinging a broom at a squirrel, and grinned. "And Creed drove by. Judy said he turned on to Main Street and was headed our direction. If he was headed home, he's probably at his boat by now."

"Okay." Kat peered into the dark, but the dock where Creed kept his boat was mostly hidden by a patch of jutting trees. "I think I see a light on in his boat." She squinted harder, not sure if she could wait any longer. Last night, after she and Lei finished their margaritas, Kat had booked a flight home for the morning. Then Lei helped her pack for the weekend. Today, Kat had spent most of her day traveling and thinking about what she'd say when she saw Creed. Now the time was here. But only if Creed would listen.

"You want me to go over there and check?" Joyce asked. "I'll tell him to get his butt in gear and get over to the sandbar 'cause you have something to say."

Kat chuckled, knowing her Mom would put on her slippers and be out the door in two seconds. "No, Mom. You stay put. I don't need you out tromping through the woods in the middle of the night. I'll just give him a little more time to—" Kat's breath caught in her throat.

"What was that?" Joyce asked. "You okay?"

"I see a spotlight." Kat swallowed. There was a bright light that appeared behind the patch of trees Kat had been staring at for hours. She stood, trying to get a better look. The light shimmered between trunks and leaves. Then it drifted out onto the still water. Kat gasped again. "It's Creed.

He's coming." The spotlight highlighted the front of Creed's boat—the deck that Thelma had dived off.

"Well, it's about time," Joyce said with cheer in her voice. "You two kids talk it out. Be brave. Tell him how you feel. I've got a hunch he feels the same."

"Thanks, Mom. I love you."

"Love you too, sweetie."

Kat set her phone down on the picnic basket and walked to the water's edge. Her bare feet pressed into wet sand. Away from the fire, the brisk night air brushed her skin. She was wearing Creed's sweatshirt, the one she'd borrowed this past week. She'd "forgotten" to give it back. Tucking her hands into the long sleeves, she wore them like mittens and watched the boat near. With the spotlight glaring, she couldn't see Creed, but figured he could see her. Nerves bundled in her stomach. She started bouncing in place, wishing he'd get to shore faster.

When the boat finally slid through the shallows and beached on the shoreline, Kat stopped bouncing. The spotlight turned off, and Creed killed the engine. He walked out of the shadows and stood at the deck railing. Moonlight spilled over his classically handsome features and flannel-clad broad shoulders.

"Hi," Kat said, wanting to run through the water and climb into his arms.

"Hi," he replied. "What are you doing out here?"

"Waiting for you."

He tipped his head like he hadn't heard her. "Aren't you supposed to be in Chicago?"

"Uh huh." Her heart pitter-pattered. "But I needed to talk to you, and you weren't answering your phone."

"I didn't have my phone."

"I figured that out when I broke into your house and saw it sitting on your kitchen counter."

Creed smirked. Then he hopped off the deck and splashed through the lake in his boots and jeans. He walked straight for her. "I listened to your message."

Kat nodded, not waiting for him to say another word. She wanted to make sure Creed knew exactly what was on her heart and her mind. "I'm not getting back together with Michael. I never intended to. I broke it off with him because my heart belonged to someone else. My heart has *always* belonged to you." She reached out a hand, unfurling it from the sweatshirt sleeve. *His* sweatshirt sleeve. Creed took it. "I shouldn't have lied to you. Or anyone else. I should've told you the truth from the first moment I saw you." She should've never put that ring back on.

"Your heart has always belonged to me?" Creed asked tentatively, skipping over the mention of her lie like it was yesterday's news.

"I've never stopped thinking of you. My feelings for you are stronger than anything I've ever felt for another man. I only used the ring as a crutch because I was scared to let myself love you again."

Creed's chest stilled. He stopped breathing.

Kat continued, wanting to get it all out before fear gobbled her up again. "I shut you out of my life because I couldn't take any more pain. I didn't know how to grieve Sarah, so I ran from everything that reminded me of her. I ran from this place. From my family. From you." She laced her fingers through his, looking for courage. "I mislabeled distance for safety. I didn't realize I left behind the people that would help me heal . . . the most important people in my life. And I'm sorry for that." Her heart thudded against her ribs. "But I don't want to run anymore. I want to be right here. With you."

Creed reached for her other hand. He found her fingers hidden in the sleeve and took hold. He grasped both her hands tightly. "You've never left my heart or my mind, Kat. *Never.* This is exactly where I want to be too." Creed swallowed, looking her in the eye with an intensity that made her knees wobbly. "And now I know why you don't want me to ride broncs."

Kat blinked. Behind her a piece of wood fell in the fire, turning to ash and coals. "Because I care about you? Because I don't want you to get hurt? Because I can't picture my life without you?" His green eyes widened at her last question, but Kat also knew how much heart and soul Creed put into rodeo. If she was going to give her heart to Creed, she needed to love all of him. "But I also understand how much you love rodeo, and I won't ask you to give up something you love. Not on my account. I just want you to be safe."

Creed nodded slowly, lapping up her words. "Do you want to know why I don't want to ride broncs anymore?"

Kat would've stumbled if he hadn't been holding her hands. "Why *you* don't?"

Creed tugged her in until they were toe to toe on the wet sand. Kat tilted back to look him in the eye.

Creed dipped his head to meet her stare. "Because I never want to hurt you. Not ever again. I never want to be the reason for your pain or tears. I can't chance that happening. I *won't* chance that happening. Not again." He tightened his grip on her hands. "This whole week, all I could think about was you. It didn't matter what I did. Nothing took your place in my head or in my heart. I don't love anything as much as I love you."

Goosebumps prickled over Kat's skin. She raised their intertwined hands and set them on Creed's chest. "You don't love anything as much as you love me?"

"Nope." Creed gathered her hands between his. His large grip engulfed hers. "I've been addicted to whiskey, tequila, and broncs, but you're the only addiction I've never been able to kick. You're the only addiction I've never *wanted* to quit."

Kat thought she might take off, soar into the sky. She grasped Creed, making sure she didn't float away. "I want this to be our time. I want to be with you *now*. I love you, Creed Sheridan. Always have."

Creed's eyes bore into hers. "Can you say it again?"

"I love you, Creed Sheridan," Kat said through a smile.

"Again?"

Kat laughed. She tipped her head back. "I love you, Creed Sheridan!" She yelled it to the stars in the sky, to the fish in the lake, to all of Maple Bay.

When her gaze fell back to Creed's, he said, "I love you too, Kat Weston."

Kat flushed, warmth running from her fingertips to her bare toes. "Will you kiss me already?" She went up on her tiptoes. "Or do I have to dare you?"

Creed barely let her finish her sentence. His lips found hers. His strong arms wrapped around her.

She was home.

EPILOGUE

Kat parked Creed's truck and got out, pulling the laundry basket across the bench seat with her. Setting the basket full of clothes on her hip, she closed the door and turned to look at her house. *Their house.* The house she and Creed had bought together. It was the cutest house she'd ever seen. It needed work, but they'd both fallen in love with it the second they saw it. The house was a two-story A-frame with big windows that looked out onto the lake. From the back of the house, it was a stone's throw to their very own dock where they kept the houseboat. So, technically, Kat and Creed had two houses. One on land. The other on water. The best of both worlds. But Kat's most favorite thing about their recent purchase was the barn and pasture off to the side.

Kat whistled as she walked toward the house. Diesel was in the pasture, nibbling at a mound of hay. At Kat's whistle, he raised his handsome head and whinnied. His black-and-white coat was thick and fuzzy, ready for upcoming winter weather. She wanted to snuggle up to him.

"Hey, sweeties! I'll bring you guys carrots after I put this laundry away," Kat called.

Diesel nickered one more time. Then he went back to munching on his hay. He was good-naturedly sharing his lunch with his new friend, a chestnut gelding named Bandit. Bandit looked curiously at Diesel, as if to ask what Diesel was talking about.

"I'll be back in a few minutes!" She smiled, glad the two geldings were getting along marvelously.

She and Creed had moved Diesel and Bandit from her parents' barn a week ago, after closing on their new house. The house was a fixer-upper, but the barn and pasture were move-in ready. Plus, Diesel and Bandit had already gotten to know each other at her parents' place. When Creed made the decision to give up riding broncs, he quickly pivoted to focusing on roping. Like bronc riding, he'd been roping since he was in high school. However, he'd never had his own horse. Creed had always borrowed a horse from the Westons. Now he had his own—Bandit. Come spring, she and Creed planned to hit the rodeo circuit together. Kat couldn't wait. Maybe eventually she'd even get a youngster herself, get back into barrel racing and poles. For now, she was enjoying trail rides and general love-and-snuggle sessions with Diesel.

Kat opened the front door. "Honey, I'm home!" she called as she slipped through the doorway, laundry basket in tow. Both she and Creed had been greeting each other like that since the purchase of their home last week. Every time, it made her giggle.

"And you brought clean underwear." Creed smiled from the middle of their torn-apart kitchen. The kitchen cabinets were mostly detached from the wall and mangled on the floor. He set down his sledgehammer and walked over to greet her with a kiss. His warm lips defrosted hers. Then he took the laundry basket so she was free to take off her coat, hat, and mittens. "It might look scary now, but I promise you'll love the cabinets I'm making for you."

"For us." Kat shimmied out of her coat.

"For us," Creed repeated. They shared a smile.

"They'll be gorgeous. I know it." She gave Creed another kiss. "Right, fur babies?" Kat addressed their little family. All three fur babies were napping on the only piece of living room furniture they had so far—the loveseat which had previously been in the houseboat. Thelma and Louise were snuggled in a blanket on the cushions. They wiggled their bodies at Kat's question, though they didn't get out of their warm cocoon. Kat didn't blame them. They loved it when Creed wrapped them up and snuggled them into the couch. Kat loved it too. Sasquatch meowed from his spot on top of the couch. Kat walked over and greeted them each with a head-scratch and a kiss. Their fur babies got along now, though Thelma still liked to chase Sasquatch from time to time. However, Sasquatch quickly learned that he held all the cards. If he stopped running and turned toward Thelma with a hiss, Thelma turned into a big wimp and ran off. It was their game of cat and mouse. Kat wasn't sure who was the mouse.

"Oh, boy. Is this what I think it is?" Creed set down the laundry basket. He grabbed the big green thermos that was tucked in with the clothes. "Is this your mom's mulled apple cider?"

"Sure is." Kat opened one of the unpacked boxes and found two mismatched mugs. "Would you like some?"

Kat and Creed didn't have a washer or dryer yet, so Kat had been doing their laundry at her parents' house. Luckily, her parents lived just a mile down the road. And Joyce always sent her home with a treat. Today, it was hot cider.

Creed unscrewed the top from the thermos. Kat offered up the mugs, and Creed filled them. Then he set the thermos on the floor and took a mug from Kat.

"How about a toast?" Creed held up his mug. A curl of blond hair stuck to his sweaty forehead. Dust was smeared across his black T-shirt. He looked beyond handsome, and Kat thought she might set down her mug and accost him in their mangled kitchen.

"To happy endings," he said.

"And new beginnings," Kat added, still in awe that she got both.

They clicked their mugs and gingerly sipped the steaming, spiced cider.

Kat's eyes fluttered at the gulp of warm decadence. *Cinnamon. Sweet. A hint of citrus.* Her mom's cider was pure perfection. "One day Mom will be able to make her famous cider in my very own crockpot. I can't wait."

Creed licked cider off his lips. "You've got the meeting with Lei's uncle on Monday, right? In Minneapolis?"

"Yep. Signing the final paperwork, and then we'll be off and running."

"I'm so proud of you," Creed grinned. "My little go-getter."

Kat grinned back. After she'd professed her love to Creed, she made it through exactly one more week as national sales manager for *Genius Appliances.* Kat had *thought* she'd wanted that job, that the position would give her a platform to have her ideas heard, to get out of the hamster wheel she was on. Instead, the hamster wheel moved faster, and *Genius Appliances* put more on her plate. A lot more. And what was she getting from all her hard work? A paycheck and no personal life. Kat didn't want that. What she wanted was to move back to Maple Bay and start a life worth living. But she also didn't want to give up her career. So, before Kat quit, Lei and Kat spent an entire night scouring the internet for job opportunities in northern Minnesota. Unfortunately, there weren't a lot of corporate sales positions outside of Minneapolis and St. Paul, and after a long night and a particularly large bowl of chocolate-peanut-butter ice cream, Kat spurted out that she and Lei should start their own business. They should make their own appliances. Kat could manage the business. Lei could engineer the products. Between the two of them, they had the skills to figure it out. They just needed the money to do so.

Kat threw out the idea on a whim, but Lei surprised her by saying she was totally in.

Kat and Lei quit *Genius Appliances* on the same day, and they quickly found an investor for their business. Lei had a wealthy uncle who was excited to invest in his niece. Now, Kat and Lei were starting their own company, *HomeStewed*— a line of vintage-inspired appliances that brought cooking back to the basics. Nothing fancy. No strange gadgets. Just quality, affordable, simple appliances that allowed families to cook with love. A crockpot was the first product they would focus on. Kat had promised her mother it wouldn't look like a spaceship.

"That deserves another cheer," Creed said, and they clinked their mugs again. "And now that you're home, I've got a surprise for you upstairs."

Kat quirked an eyebrow, knowing that the only room upstairs was the loft bedroom. She smirked suggestively.

"Not that kind of surprise," Creed chuckled. "Come on." He took her hand and led her upstairs.

"What do you have up your sleeve?"

Creed pushed open the door. The bedroom was sunny, warm, and bright. The back wall was all glass with a view of the lake, but other than the priceless view, the room was mostly empty. So far, they had a mattress and a lamp. Both sat on the well-worn orange shag carpet.

But then Kat noticed something new in their bedroom. A wooden chest sat next to the windows.

Creed squeezed her hand. "I made you a hope chest."

"What?" she croaked, nearly spilling the cider she still held. "You made that? For me?"

He nodded, and they walked over to the chest. Its glossy wood shone in the sunlight. Kat squatted down, setting her mug on the shag carpet so both her hands were free. She ran her fingers over the antique lock on the front. A lump gathered in her throat.

"It's cedar wood," Creed said. "The perfect place to keep blankets or photos or whatever you like." He knelt beside her, placing his mug on the carpet as well.

"It's absolutely beautiful," she said, trying not to cry. "Thank you."

Creed opened the chest. On the underside of the lid were dates burned into the wood. Kat knew exactly what each date represented.

The date they first met. When Kat was a sassy twelve-year-old and scolded Creed for doing a crappy job of cleaning stalls.

The date of their first kiss. Kat's senior year and the summer she'd never forget.

The date Creed found Kat and her rental car stuck in the muddy field. The day they started their journey back to each other.

The date they bought their first house together. Just last week.

And, then there was today's date.

Kat looked at Creed, overwhelmed with emotion.

"What's today?" she asked, speaking past the lump lodged in her throat.

Creed's forest-green eyes sparked. "There's something on the bottom of the chest as well."

Kat tipped forward and peeked inside. At the bottom of the chest, there was a small black box. When Creed reached into the chest and grabbed it, she thought she might pass out. Instead, she made an incredibly embarrassing choking sound. She looked at Creed. He laughed, already on one knee.

"Kat?" He popped open the little black box. Inside was a gold band with three diamonds inlaid. "You are the toughest, sweetest woman I've ever known, and I don't want to chance losing you ever again. I want us to have a life together. I want to laugh and cry with you. I want to be your rock. I want to have Sunday dinner with you. Play kickball with you even though you cheat. Ride off into the sunset with you. Every day. *Always.*" He pulled the ring out of the box. "Would you do me the honor of being my wife?

Because I can't picture my life without you. *You* are my best life."

Kat didn't know what her face or body was doing. She felt like she was in a dream or watching from a distance. But she wasn't. She was here. Creed was kneeling beside her, asking her to be his wife.

Kat placed one hand on the hope chest, steadying herself. She knew the boy Creed had been. She knew the man he'd become. And she loved them both. "Creed, you have my heart. You always have. I'm not going anywhere. I decided long ago that you are my person. YES. A big, fat *YES*."

Creed released a relieved laugh and took her left hand. He slipped the ring on her finger. The gold band felt like it was meant to be there.

Grabbing Kat into a hug, Creed rolled her onto the shag carpet and kissed her through her giggles. Kat looped her hands around Creed's neck and told him that she loved him. He stared down at her with the brightest smile she'd even seen.

In that instant, Kat knew Creed had built hope in her heart long before he ever built her a chest.

***

JOYCE'S MULLED APPLE CIDER

1 gallon fresh Apple Cider

1 orange

1 piece of ginger (about an inch in size)

5 or 6 cinnamon sticks

1 tablespoon whole cloves

A cheesecloth, kitchen twine, or a tea ball

5 quart (or larger) slowcooker

Whole Cranberries for garnish

1. Do not use a slow cooker that looks like a spaceship.
2. Pour Apple Cider into slowcooker. Turn slowcooker on to low setting.
3. Slice the orange into ¼" rounds. Give each slice a gentle squeeze before adding to slowcooker.
4. Cut ginger into ¼" pieces. Slightly grate the outside of each ginger slice (to release flavor). Add ginger to slowcooker.
5. Add cinnamon sticks to slowcooker.
6. Put the cloves in a cheesecloth (sealed with kitchen twine) or a tea ball. Add to slowcooker. You can add cloves without the cloth or tea ball, but it's easier to serve cider when they are contained & can be easily removed.

7. Cover slowcooker and cook on low for 4 hours.

8. Serve in your favorite mug and share with your favorite people.

9. Optional: add whole cranberries to each mug as a pretty garnish.

10. Enjoy!

COUNTRY STARS IN MAPLE BAY

(A Maple Bay Novel, Book 3)

Myra despises liars. And the biggest fake just stole her coffee shop.

Skyler Ridge, the famous country music star, is a fake. At least that's what the tabloids say—that he doesn't have a country bone in his body. Running from a scandal and the relentless paparazzi, Skyler lands in the small town of Maple Bay where he buys a failing coffee shop. He wants peace, quiet, and the chance to reinvent himself. Instead, he gets a cowgirl-barista with a surly attitude. But even though Myra drives him crazy, he can't deny the fire she lights in him—a spark he hasn't felt in years.

Single-mother Myra is edging on forty and has no room for a man in her life. She barely has room to breathe. But when she can't save her coffee shop from foreclosure, the most irritatingly handsome man forces himself into her life. And she wants him out. *Now*. So when Skyler's agent presents

Myra with a deal to gain her coffee shop back, she jumps at the chance.

The catch? Myra must turn Skyler into a real cowboy and save his country music career—before his label drops him. But there's a reason Skyler ended up in Maple Bay. A secret he needs to unravel. And he's not leaving until he finds the truth. Whether Myra likes it or not.

A sweet enemies-to-lovers romance full of hope, redemption, and how following your heart will always lead you home.

Sign up for Brittney's newsletter to be notified of each new release:

http://www.brittneyjoybooks.com/newsletter

Author's Note
Brittney Joy

As an author, I sometimes get asked where I get the inspiration for my stories. As a reader, I think this is one of the most interesting things to learn from other writers. So, I thought I'd share a little insight with you as to where my inspiration comes from.

For me, inspiration comes in many forms, but often it's something from my real life that will spur my imagination. None of my stories or characters are based completely on real-life. However, while I am writing, I'm often more aware of my surroundings. As a writer, I think my brain is always grinding over story ideas. I also keep a notebook *just* for plot ideas that pop into my head—from a news story, a conversation I had with a friend, or even something shared on social media.

Second Chance in Maple Bay simply started with a character idea. I kept picturing a woman that had run away from her hometown because she couldn't face the death of a loved one. That was all I knew when I first had the idea for this story. Then, as I wrote the first book in the Maple Bay

Series, the puzzle pieces started to fall into place. Kat started to form in my head, based on the characters I was creating in *Starting Over in Maple Bay (book 1)*. Plus, I immediately fell in love with Creed in book one, even though he only made a few short appearances. I knew I needed to tell his story.

Some writers are "plotters." They outline their whole story, chapter by chapter, before they ever start writing. Some writers are "pantsers." They sit down and start writing and discover the characters and story as they type away. I fall somewhere in the middle. When I start a new book, I spend a few weeks figuring out my characters through free-writing about their past. As I get to understand the characters better, I'll also start to figure out the main plot points. Essentially, before I start writing the first draft, I know the beginning of the story, the end, and a few major twists along the way. Then, as I write, the rest of the story gets filled in.

Here are a few tidbits from my real life or my past that helped to inspire certain areas of Kat and Creed's story...

Thelma and Louise are highly inspired by two special dogs in my life. Louise is literally my dog (Lucy) in the written word. She may be the only character I've ever written that is exactly true to life. My real-life dog, Lucy, is a terrier-chihuahua mix. My husband and I adopted her over ten years ago (she was a stray) and she has been my permanent sidekick since. She's choosey about who she loves but loves *her people* with blind loyalty. She is a professional cuddler and thinks she is much bigger than her thirteen-pound body. I don't know what I'd do without her. And, Thelma is based on one of my best friend's dogs—a very rascally Jack Russell.

Cheese curds are one of my favorite things to get at the Minnesota State Fair . . . my husband restores trucks and has a 1985 black Chevy dually that he lovingly refers to as *The Cowboy Cadillac* . . . in high school, I worked at a drive-in diner that had the best homemade root beer . . . my hometown has an amazing bakery with *to-die-for* maple bars . . . I have spent many Minnesota-summers on boats and sandbars . . .

So, I guess what I'm trying to say is that inspiration comes in many forms. If you are looking for it, it'll find you.

Thank you so much for joining me in Maple Bay. I hope Kat and Creed's journey warmed your heart and made you smile.

Sending you love and best wishes,
Brittney

www.brittneyjoybooks.com

If you have a few minutes, I'd love your honest review of Second Chance in Maple Bay on Amazon, GoodReads, or anywhere you purchased your book. Reviews help me understand what stories readers enjoy. They also help me decide what to write next. Please leave a review if you'd like to see more of Maple Bay.

Books by Brittney Joy

Sweet Young Adult Contemporary:
Lucy's Chance (Red Rock Ranch, book 1)
Showdown (Red Rock Ranch, book 2)
Rodeo Daze (Red Rock Ranch, book 3)

Young Adult Fantasy:
OverRuled (The OverRuled Series, book 1)
OverRun (The OverRuled Series, book 2)
OverThrown (The OverRuled Series, book 3)

Sweet Adult Romance:
Starting Over in Maple Bay (book 1)
Second Chance in Maple Bay (book 2)
Country Stars in Maple Bay (book 3)

www.brittneyjoybooks.com

Made in the USA
Monee, IL
28 March 2022